GATHERINGS

The En'owkin Journal of First North American Peoples

VOLUME IV

RE-GENERATION:

EXPANDING THE WEB TO CLAIM OUR FUTURE

Fall, 1993

Theytus Books, Penticton, British Columbia

GATHERINGS:
The En'owkin Journal of First North American Peoples

Volume IV - 1993

Published annually by Theytus Books Ltd. and the En'owkin Centre for the En'owkin International School of Writing

A catalogue will be mailed upon request.

Please inquire about our advertising rates and contributors' guidelines.

Please send submissions and letters to 'Gatherings', c/o En'owkin Centre, 257 Brunswick Street, Penticton, B.C. V2A 5P9 Canada. All submissions must be accompanied by self-addressed stamped envelope (SASE). Manuscripts without SASEs may not be returned. We will not consider previously published manuscripts or visual art.

Typeset by Theytus Books Ltd. Printed and bound in Canada

ISSN 1180-0666
ISBN 0-919441-48-3

TABLE OF CONTENTS

Section II - SPIRIT

Section III - SOCIETY

EDITORIAL

There are rare moments in the interactions of everyday when something deep within connects with the "spirit-stuff" of others and a new friendship is birthed. Some fade in infancy, but enough mature to make the journey a shared experience. It is the collective need to share intimacy with others that separates man from the other primates, and when need is lacking, becomes symptomatic of neuroses. Friendships define our existence, take us beyond our ego boundaries, and sensitize us so that it becomes possible to touch a leper, smile with our elders, feel the hunger of Ethiopia, the pain of Bosnia, and the joy of children. It is always a growth experience, and though the encounters be singular or many, we take some portion of the "Spirit-stuff" onward.

As a young Métis, I spent many long and joyful hours in the company of many friends exploring the texture of Saskatchewan. Many friends remain so today, though time and distance have exacted their tolls. But the most enduring of friends have been those forged while lying prone, face down to the open pages of some book, fingers screwed into both ears to prevent sound from intruding into my literary sanctuary. My family, although large, is fractured due to poverty and alcohol, and all had to leave home at an early age. My familial condition is not unlike that of many Métis. Unlike our reserve brethren, we did not have physical boundaries to contain us and make us familiar one to another. Survival is long, hard and scattered work in a society that discriminates without protection. When the events of my life overpowered me, when the monotony of our poverty overwhelmed me, when the disconnectedness of my cultural condition overcame me, my friends were there, offering escape, travel, excitement and spiritual succor.

Through school and on, I have been sustained by such friends. They allowed me to transcend the travail of formal education and have shared the meanderings of existence. Like many Métis before and since, I left the province of my birth and never went back. Connections to my home province were severed further when my parents got too old to work and moved away. Retirement would be too pretentious a word to ascribe to my farm laborer father who put in his last full crop for someone else at the age of 85 (how does one retire from poverty?), or my mother who spent the best years of her life on her knees, scrubbing the floors of the rich white folks in our small town. Those knees must have been hard for I remember many hours of early childhood spent in kneed prayer in reaction to whatever priestly penances and supplications implored. There is no one more fervent in ritual than a Métis Catholic woman spooked by the hell constructed by the latest black-skirted purveyor of the book and beads. They are gone now, my father first and my mother just last fall. "I never knew I could pray with a drum," she cried to a cousin shortly before her death. Too often the important things of life are found too late to be savored!

With such thoughts, I invite you, the reader, to embark on a new journey. In the following passages you will meet new friends and renew old acquaintances. Shared experiences , as a representation of the primacy of our lives, make for smooth renewals and new intimates. For the once disconnected, the writers give strength to explore heritage, to define roots and inspiration to fight for social justice and equity. Within, your persona will be nurtured, refuged, and sanctuaried. In The Road Less Travelled, Peck defines love as "the will to extend one's self for the purpose of nurturing one's own or another's spiritual growth." Santayana said, "One's friends are that part of the human race with which one can be human." This is a human book. Writing and reading are evolutionary acts beyond our ego boundaries, whereby, through reciprocal acts of caring and nurturing we construct human kind.

Don Fiddler
Penticton, 1993

SELF

"ON SEEING YOU AGAIN"

I sat on a wicker lounger with Che-Chu or Jesus Angel Perez Valverde, in The Pitt Gallery on Vancouver's eastside, the opening night of his, "New Roots of the Same Skin."

The cavernous intensity of the indigo splash gallery writhes to the rhythm of its adherents, inside the music, smoke, sound and heat of festive ambience. The mood is paganistic, the pulse savage; me and Che-Chu, we like it here!

My Mexican "bro" and I had been introduced the day before by the lovely and elegant Director of the gallery, Dana Claxton, and so our second meeting was like the first one, a mere formality.

And tonight, here we sit, two aboriginal men, two indigenous men of this island called Turtle; smoking, watching, observing. Two souls of the same skin, two skins of the same soul; two artists bent on sanity, two lives imitating art.

Che-Chu and I first tried to converse in our two colonial languages, Spanish and English; with no measurable success, but a great amount of gesticulating and gesturing, like Columbus and the first 'Indios' who saved his miserable hide.

I was trying to tell him about the profound effect his art had on me, he was trying to explain his craft in terms of medium and form- this much we were able to convey.

Finally we just sat and communicated as all 'indios' do all over Turtle Island. Communication that is silent but salient, understated, with a wicked undercurrent of humour. A mutual awareness of the absurd in the ordinary, catching the obtuse and reveling in the ridiculous. Usually innate, sometimes superficial, but always loaded with the ironic or the succinctly irreverent.

Eventually I go to the bar and buy us two cokes, the soft drink kind, liquid. I hand one to Che-Chu and assure him, "No spirits!" He caught that right away, "Si, no spirits". We both laugh.

We sit some more and watch the dancers dance and those not touched by rhythm dance even harder.

By the by this lady comes up and offers Che-Chu a beer. They go into a long tirade about the can, she in halting Spanish, he in flowing poetry of Latin American idiom. Finally she gives up and waddles away into the distant dark. My buddy shows me the can, its Coors Light, he can't read the English labelling. "Spirits" he queries. "Spirits!" I intone. We both laugh and resume our watch.

Che-Chu communicates best through his art. His brush speaks. It talks of an elementary sojourn into the "Pan-American" world experience. The world of fascism, poverty, oppression, genocide. It speaks of dreams that dared to be dreamt, and hopes dashed against the buttressed void of greed, capitalism, and materialism.

With infernal strokes of his brush he creates subliminal juxtapositions of prostitutes and angels, gunships and crucifixes, syringes and skulls, subways and cowboys... flashes of the perverse; statements of the sublime.

His pieces leap out at you in neon montages of consummate fury and indigence. But there is no hate, there is no acceptance, there is only reality and renewal.

Che-chu's art is defiant, intense, indomitable.

I like Che-Chu's art.

It is an invaluable fact of life that whenever two Indians come into contact, there is an immediate and pervasive sense of identity and definable sense of acceptance, an implicit sense of community.

Whether in an elevator, a mall or street, two Indians seldom encounter each other without giving, without sharing, without receiving strength, power, validation.

How many times, in my propensity to travel and explore, my path will cross, connect, touch, converge on circles of other Indians at borrowed places like elevators, hotels, airports, restaurants, malls, stores. In little towns, big cities, gas stations, train stations, bus stops, bars, streets and skid row.

And yet I am never amazed or taken back when he or she says hello, "tansi", howdy or whatever seems appropriate at the time, or totally inappropriate, for that matter, period. I find it good, I find it empowering; a celebration, like a good joke. A ceremony almost, like a bad joke.

The journey becomes intuitive, familiar, sociable, spirited. People. Source. Being.

It was at a conference on the East Coast; I walked into an elevator (elevators are such great metaphors for society), and there's four 'bros' staring back at me, sombre, poker-faced, but already I could feel a palpable energy of mirth, of the need for diversion. We go up one floor, the door opens and in walks another 'bro' with the most ghastly headdress we have ever witnessed on this side of the Rockies. He steps in, nods to us, turns and we start to ascend two more floors. Before the door has fully shut, everyone is already glancing at each other and "having a good time".

One of the guys started to needle the new arrival about whether he's a bird or indeed a chief.

Everyone has a good laugh including the Chief, as he alights onto the fourth floor, to contemplate far weightier and pressing matters, than five guys in an elevator. The rest of us get off on the sixth floor, congenial and laughing easily, five guys who didn't know each other, but in the time it took an elevator to travel six floors, we had arrived upon a common ground.

Our meetings take on great meaning and imparts its own brand of honour, respect, dignity, those touchstones of our "Indianness". Our meetings become microcosms of our society, strong, full, free, lively. Tractable; Intractable.

On another occasion, I was flying back from the East (I don't know why it's always East to West), and I snagged a seat next to an old high school friend, an Ojibway.

Within meal distance into the flight we started talking about what we were going to eat when we got home. He rhapsodies at great lengths about chunks of meat from "free ranging cows" stewed into a broth of carrots and macaroni. I throw in other associated condiments, and even more "free ranging" chunks of moose meat with celery. Right on schedule, the stewardess (appropriately enough) plunks a pasty-colored, crescent-shaped, lonely chunk of bagel (we Indians call them beagles), in front of him. But he, not being Sioux, misses a beat, but not timing, as he exclaims in a timbre used only by men saved from drowning, "Look bro, a big macaroni!"

And so we go about our journeys, doting upon each twist and turn, laughing at the minuscule, guffawing at the subtleties, taking in the big picture, splicing the big picture.

But always aware and expectant of the next turn, the closing of one circle, the beginning of another. The short distances between meetings, the gatherings, and the far distances between actual horizons and potential mirages.

One time I flew (West to East and then Southwest, like a crow!), three thousand miles to get away from it all, work, stress, the familiar.

The next morning, I go down to the lobby, to plan my retreat and my self-indulgence. I buy a paper, light a smoke and sink into the nearest couch. With the absolute mastery of timing that only another Indian can appreciate, since we are so in tune to it, a voice from behind me plummets, "Tansi boy, what are you doing here?!" I almost expected to hear the inevitable, "When are you going home?!" of Indians on the road.

Actually I was tempted to ask him that myself. It was one of my best friends and colleagues, there to M.C. a pow-wow, one of the many honourable traditions that would put an Indian on the road.

I explained to him my malady and my search for a possible antidote. He gave me his prognosis and said, "Come on I'll help you!"

For the rest of the week the subject never came up again. I was cured. He was cured!

Our paths are like that. Us Indians, unencumbered by time, space, or levity.

But there is also pain, sadness, sorrow we feel for our brothers and sisters. The kind of helpless tone you feel when you come from din sum and you see a 'bro' scrounging around in the dumpster for scraps to keep him on his feet. A deep helpless shit of a nauseating feeling that comes from your stomach and your pen hurts to write about it. The kind of hurt which makes you feel dead and the dictum, "power comes from the end of a gun," takes a magnified credence and truism.

But hey, we shan't discuss that. After all, this is a civilized country, and the great illusion of the noblesse oblige must be shared up against pride and prejudice... at all costs.

Che-Chu and I never saw each other again (yet) after that opening night. But for a few immutable hours, we became brothers. We shared a kinship, a bond, a perspective as to "where we'd been and where we were headed."

With unspoken knowledge we could convey our "Indianness" to each other, our separate path and still our common destination.

The invisible thread of our connectedness that spanned a continent and without a word being spoken, we had "seen with the same eyes".

And our eyes spoke the same language. An old language of pure power and sheer elegance.

A language which speaks with intimacy about history and tradition. About Mother Earth. An enduring language which speaks with immediacy about spirit, about prophecy, about healing. A respectful language speaking about Elders, the sacred teachings and about "the" guardianship.

A language not constrained by boundaries, immune to age, absolved of time. A language comfortable with the intangible inside the intangible; the silence between the silence; where space and time are of one essence and of one reality. Where past, present and future converge and coalesce.

The language of the Indian eye acknowledges the already cognizant, speaking with a perception beyond the mere perceptive. Poignant. Benign.

It is a language not readily understood by the outside. To us it conveys and embodies the sharing of the sacrosanct, our inner strength.

You cannot understand it if you have never been "the wretched of the Earth," the brown nigger of the Americas. You cannot comprehend it if you have never been deprived of human dignity, respect or simple decency.

You will not hear it or see it spoken in someone else's eyes, if you have never been denied your land, your culture, your spirituality, your children or your tongue.

You will never understand it because it is too subtle, too sharp, too illogical, too human.

But most of all you will never be able to contain it, appropriate it, supress it, or destroy it.

Spider webs are such a phenomena. So intricate, so prolific, so delicate and yet so strong. Swaying to the slightest breeze, tenacious in the greatest wind.

In it's humble purpose are strands of commonality, connections of collectivity. It is at once fragile to the human eye, but intransigent to its elemental "being".

SPEAKING THOSE NAMES

aloud
speaking those names
you have given me
calling myself by those names
in just that voice that you have spoken
hearing myself in those names
each time
I become again myself
my holding-your-hand self
my hair braided, round cheeked self
my barefoot, fringed cut-off self
my lace tights, Easter hat self,
my watermelon loving, woodtick hating self,
my child self, my teen-age self, my now self
my whole self
I hear myself in those names
being pulled back by those names
know again myself in relationship

aloud
mustoord
kim-a-dill
lady
tim-ber-ly
speaking them out loud in rescue
hearing them out loud in your voice
mine sunshine
you can hear some of these kimbee
come on my girl
knowing by those names who I was
to you
to myself

becoming again those names
sister
white head
the brain
mimmie
being claimed again in names
spoken then
named across time
k-k
across death
kimmie
across change
dr.
hearing you call
kiii-iiimmm
claiming myself
in speaking those names
aloud

MISHOMIS

I don't want to live
without the memory of you
I don't want the dream
of tracing the outline of your feet
to end before I die

I dream of your songs
I dream of you singing
I dream of the way your voice sounded
I dream of the way you told the stories
of each song
in the fading light of evening
where they came from
who dreamed them
who taught them to you
when you were young

I haven't forgotton
what you said
When you going to sing
you sing at least four songs eh
When you going to sing
you go through that song
at least four times eh
at least four times
Don't take no medicine when you sing eh

Once you take that medicine to help you sing
you have to take it all the time after eh

You take it
you have to take it all the time eh

I haven't forgotten
what you said
I have only taken the medicine
of your memory
of your memory
of your memory
of your memory.

RAIN

Roaring down
on cars and windows
Trying to get in.
Flooding all the roads
and dancing through the sky.
Making a swimming pool
out of my front yard.
Splashing in the puddles.

Kyle Sam

POWWOW DAYS

This summer or early spring
  it was powwow time again.
Straightening out my outfit
  and straightening out my yarn.
During times I practice moves
  to get the beat for tonight.
I listen to tapes of my favorite
  drum groups to learn their songs.
I want to be ready for Grand Entry and
  all intertribals.......
Once the powwow starts, I shake hands
  with all my friends from near and far.
My contest is about to start, I feel
  kind of shaky........
When I'm dancing, I like to move all over
  to the songs that I learned from my tapes.
Once the contest is over, I feel like I'm
  gonna fall over.
When the powwow is over, I meet my friends
  and we play all over.

FURIOUS ADMIRES THE CLOUDS

Furious admires the clouds
and seasonings remark a broadbased effort
sparkling to the ugliness
how can you not inhale her loneliness?

stretching out to zero
plussed and sleeping spaced out
never watching but talking with a beat
one two

warming up to ripside
and practising scales into an empty orange juice can
the critics weren't doing that and
gritty
ramming up against your language
I let it all out

GIFT OF STONE

Once, upon a sandy beach
miniature dunes etched by wind
were a written record of waters
  a half mile distant.

A trickle from a nearby mountain
was mother to a grove of willows
which dry-clattered their branches
  for most of the year.

A terrible stench permeated all
within this shaded stand, the putrid
odors of creatures whose task
  is devouring the dead.

These feared-by-many vultures
brood and belch here, communicating
by scent, flapping heavily away
  when summoned by death.

At the edge of this haven, circling
to avoid its foulness, I saw
lying in the sand like an offering
  a carefully crafted stone.

A weight, designed to absorb water
and sink nets in this desert lake,
perhaps detached and lost here
  when this was an island sea.

I carried it in awe and respect,

this treasure given only once,
to drop into deep blue waters
  returning the gift to the giver.

I raised my eyes to the mountains
and studied ancient beach lines
hundreds of feet above, standing
  there beneath a former sea.

I thanked the vultures for detouring
my steps, I thanked the rains for
nourishing the lake. I thanked the
  hands which fashioned the gift.

I built a small fire and spent
the night star-gazing, in wonder
that the vast universe can be
  mirrored in a silent lake.

Carlson Vicenti

VAN

Slicing through the darkness of sleep
dividing the fog of my dreams
an arrow of geese
honk honk honk by

I wake in an unlit hotel room
open the curtain that separates me
from the world

I focus on Vancouver
and a cold gray dismal rain
The geese are travelling North
They don't see familiar landmarks
now they use streets as a guide
and fly unhindered by traffic lights
above Granville boulevard

The city awakens to pile drivers
pounding stakes into mother earth
I see the land paved and lifeless
clothed by concrete and black tar asphalt
her naked beauty covered
her soft blanket of trees gone
her mountains torn apart
and rebuilt into square symmetric towers

In the glowing blur of neon lights
homeless souls beg for money
crazy babblers talk to themselves
stoners and drunks look for a fix
high heeled prostitutes wiggle their bootie

bidding for a buck
a jelly doughnut brain cop
stands on the corner
trying to look intimidating

I focus on a rain drop
gliding down the window
I know my ancestors are in the streams
I know my ancestors are in the air
I know my ancestors are in the ground
and I hear their light footsteps
in the steady drizzle that falls

Carlson Viceni

SPOTTED LAKE

circles of water
craddled in the arms
of mother earth
hundreds of round mirrors
reflecting the past
and the future
my eyes walk through a maze of dreams
that connect my spirit
to my surroundings
a woman's eyes sparkle
each pool captures warm shafts of light
penetrating turbulent clouds
that swirl above
red tail hawk glides on the wind's song
and magpies black and white wings
dance to the same melody
at my feet
pools are medicine wheels
compressed to eclipses in the distance
dreams squeezed tightly
releasing a snow capped mountain
that looks over us
a car passes
and the doppler shift draws me back
to where we're perched
overlooking a day
that lingers like the smell of sage
in my mind

MY FATHER

My father
drew a green chalk circle
in a small space
in the black driveway.
He filled the circle with marbles,
then taught us how to play,
me with my hair combed
and my friend with his wild eyes.

It was near the end of summer
and so we played with every chance we had.
We laughed and shuffled happily
on the dirty driveway
and at the end of every day
we would promise to play again,
tomorrow,
if it didn't rain.

It was a great simplicity,
until we became aware of winning and losing
and the rules we made
became bigger than we were.
Then, one day,
when we had forgotten how to play,
we took the marbles we had won
and left the circle
bare and cold
and empty.

Kevin Paul

I saw my friend, just the other day,
we're both much older now.
We laughed about the games we played
and about the childish arguments;
my hair was not combed;
the wildness
was gone from his eyes.

A VISIT WITH SHAS

Franny was a person who liked to get things done and to be where she was supposed to be on time. She was never late and always prized herself for having this attitude towards the things she strived for. One day on the way to work Franny got a flat tire and was stranded on the highway between O.K. Falls and Penticton. She was very upset about this because she had an important meeting to attend at the centre she worked at. So here she was stranded, wondering what to do.

"Well I suppose I should call the Centre. Maybe someone there will help me."

As she kept looking at the other cars going by she thought about her life going by and by this time was quite concerned about all the events in her life. Out of the blue this old man came walking towards her and said, "Hello, lady. Are you in need of some help?"

Puzzled, she glanced at him, not trusting who he was. "Ah, no. I'm fine. I'm just waiting for a friend to show up and help me with the flat tire."

She did not remove herself from the car. She was afraid this old man was a weirdo and she was ready for any kind of action. The old man sensed this and told her, "You know you shouldn't be threatened by me. I am just offering you my help, if you need it. My name is Shas. Everyone knows me around here so if you need my help I live over at that ranch over there. I just go along these roads and collect beer bottles and cans that people discard from their cars. What is your name?" He was persistant in finding out her name and offering to change the tire for her.

"Ah, my name is Franny. I live in O.K. Falls and work in Penticton." By this time Franny felt a bit more at ease about the little old man. She continued, "I have a spare tire and a jack in the trunk. Are you sure you don't mind?"

"Oh, no," the old man replied. "I have nothing else better to do and besides I don't mind helping a lady in distress!" Franny looked at him and gave a brief smile. Still having thoughts about the murderers wandering around disguising themselves as god knows who, she got out of the car and opened the trunk . Muttering away to himself, the old man Shas walked to the back of the car and took out the tire and jack. He said, "Don't be afraid of me, ma'am. I will change your tire and you will be safely on your way to the destination you are headed for."

"Oh, no, Shas. It's so nice that there are still good people in this world."

He looked at her, sensing that she was unhappy, and he decided to joke about how fast she must have been going to blow the tire off the way it did. Franny giggled a bit and realized how tense she was.

"Oh, I'm sorry. It's just that I had a deadline this morning for a meeting and now I'm late."

"Well, girl, sometimes you just have to slow down in life. This flat tire may have saved you from an accident or running into some animal who decides to cross the road. You see, sometimes life works this way. I'm an old man and believe me, these things happen that way."

Franny felt much more at ease and thought about the little white lie she told him earlier, hoping he wouldn't ask about her imaginary friend. Old Shas already knew no one was coming to her rescue. He finished changing the tire and said, "There you go, miss. Now you can continue on your journey."

"Thank you very much, " she replied. The old man collected his bottles and said, "Good luck with your deadlines!" and walked towards the highway, keeping his eyes peeled on the sides of the road for any bottles or cans he could find.

"Thanks again, Shas!" she yelled out the window.

As Franny drove back on to the highway, she thought about just how much of life that she was taking for granted and seriously felt bad for Shas because he was so kind to help her. She felt bad about the way the world was and how conditioned she was to society's way of thinking. So she decided to turn around and go back to find Shas. She entered the driveway that he said was his. She spotted Shas already on the porch of the house sorting his bottles. "Excuse me Shas! It's me, the lady with the flat tire! I just wanted to thank you again for helping me and also for giving me some insight on my life. I would like to give you some money. I hope you aren't offended in any way. I would have had to pay some guy to change my tire from a garage so I would like to give you this."

She handed him the money and he replied, "You know, lady, there ought to be more people in the world like you. Thank you very much. My wife is in the hospital in Oliver and the reason I was collecting these bottles was to buy some gas to visit."

Franny was so happy that she turned around and made his day. He also made her day. Franny gave her good wishes to the old man, feeling like a million bucks. She smiled and said to herself, "Yup, sometimes we just got to slow down in life!" As she drove to work she took a deep breath and said, "That was the best visit I ever had in a long time." It was also his name that was interesting, Shas... "Shas" in her language meant grizzly bear.

Pamela Dudoward

MEDIOCRE GUYS

These mediocre guys
with
their mediocre clothes
and
their mediocre eyes
look longingly
at me.
Circles, circles
chasing
chances;
flipping
nickels
with two-sided heads-
of course,
we wanted tails.
We keep chasing
rainbows,
the colours
bright and glaring.
Rainbows
are for watching,
gazing
admiringly-
their distance
an attraction.
Rose-coloured
glasses
we wear,
filter;
our eyes
accustomed

to the glare.
But
we still want
that rainbow,
to share
its beauty-
thinking
we will glow,
push it
deep
within our pockets
where pain is placed
and grows
in deep, dark
dungeons
and cool out
corners
where secrets
keep so well.
These
mediocre guys
with their mediocre smiles
and their mediocre ways-
they chase us,
and we chase rainbows
until
one of us
will tire.
Then
we stop
and look-
these rainbows
aren't so real.
We coloured them
with crayons

that melt
into
mediocre guys
in bars
with mediocre lives
and you
are just
another face,
another body
colouring
a picture
you'd rather
put on a fridge
than
hang in your life.
These other guys
you thought mediocre
before,
they feel warm,
they
make you feel warm
and
not for one hot moment
or
a night full
of sweat
that makes you wonder
if you were
really
there at all.
No-
these others
make you think
of tomorrow
and wonder

if they'll be there-
if you want,
even
if not forever.
Round and round
going so fast
you just might
pass the rest
and
you can almost
miss
a fateful fact-
that studs
are mediocre at best.

Melissa Pope

IN CLASS

I write their words because they are too heavy for me
to carry on my wobbling backbone in between my shoulder blades,
heavy as the green bowling ball I see hidden in the gravel
in the parking lot
I walk on everyday.

The four white women that were at the sweat, they were
pipe carriers.
One of them had shifty eyes. The other three were blue,
in front of a cold sky watching the fire rise through the
smoke.

I hear their words when I bite my lips and nails.
A concert of ignorance playing, polluting the air for our
ears. Breathing in someone else's burp or whatever else. I
didn't get up and walk out, even though I intended to.

The medicine man who could never truly be one told me
to use my hands, hold the water, carry the water, drink
the water,
and became a professional bowler.

COLD ROOMS

I like to stare out the window
the one with ugly curtains
when no one walks by
so I don't have to see what I'm missing
I will close my curtains, close my vows, hide in my sheets
around the corner, by a rock and tree and
an ambulance might come, might find me half alive
I could gain some insight.
I feel like my grandmother
she lies
in her hospital   sterile   hospital bed
fetal position
on her side
helpless and confused
almost child-like
as I am
in my bed
on my side, fetal position
I am a child
alone, closed eyes
I imagine lying within her
frail arms
in her cold sterile bed
I could smell her
soft wrinkled skin

Melissa Pope

I could see the knowledge in her eyes
and hear her strength in her breath
as it rises, as it falls
in and out of her last...
Grandmother,
your shining star grandaughter
has lost...

FROZEN THOUGHTS, FROZEN FEELINGS

It's one of the important lessons I learned a while back- you can't just keep taking in without giving back. If you do so, you're going against the laws of the Natural World. Those laws don't tolerate an imbalance.

During these years I've come to believe that we cannot envision a community of the future unless we take several conditions into consideration. One is that we can never forget that the people who occupy and rule North America have hatched some pretty terrible plans for us. Not just in the past, but in our current lifetimes.

They have deliberately sterilized at least 35% of our women. There are thousands of us who have been victims of their residential schools. There are many more thousands of us who had been the victims of their foster homes and adoption agencies. And then there is the relentless condition of racism that we face every day. All of this has combined to leave some pretty horrible scars on our spirits and lives.

These are some of the factors we discuss in the "Community Development" workshops I've designed with my partners. We analyze how these plans have affected our lives, and we examine what we need to do to heal ourselves so we can once again envision a future on our own terms.

It's night and we are driving on one of the "ice roads" that are plowed on the frozen river. This driving on a frozen river always gives me a sort of a rush. I guess it's the idea that maybe the ice will suddenly crack and we would have to make a "hell bent for leather" run to survive. Bungee jumping on a different level.

We're on our way to meet the mother of one of the workshop participants. During the session today Helen had approached me during a break and asked if she could talk to me privately. I had agreed and asked if she wanted to go outside and have a smoke since we couldn't smoke in the building.

Once we were outside, she seemed to have trouble finding a way to bring up the subject she wanted to talk about. While making the usual remarks about how cold it was, her eyes kept scanning the ground as if what she wanted to say was somehow caught in the snow.

As I stared at the snow a chain of words passed through my mind, "Frozen thought, frozen feelings" . . . the snow covers a lot of secrets.

Finally, with a heavy exhaling of smoke she began to speak. "I've had three children. After the last one I couldn't get pregnant anymore. All this time I thought there was something wrong with me. Sometimes I thought maybe God was punishing me for something." Her voice was almost a whisper; all the time she spoke she kept looking at the ground.

After a couple of seconds of silence she looked up and stared into my eyes: "The things you were saying today made me realize that maybe it's not me. Maybe they did something to me at the hospital. When I think about it, I'm not the only woman who stopped having kids. I'm going to find out what happened."

As she spoke the sound of determination entered her voice. "I'm going to get some answers. I'm going to end this not knowing."

"My mother knows about a lot of things that have happened around here," she told me in an almost conspiratorial tone. "I've told her what we have been discussing in the workshop, and she wants to meet you. Can you come over to her house tonight?"

Without a second thought I said, "Yeah, sure. But I'll need directions on how to get to her house."

"Joseph knows her house, and he would be glad to bring you over there. He's our cousin." With that we finished our smokes and went back inside to finish the rest of the workshop.

So here's Joseph and me buzzing along on the frozen Moosonee River in his four-wheeler. It's a beautiful night. Stars by the thousands, and a sliver of Grandmother Moon. I remember nights like this back home. I remember walking the silent road in the embrace of the cold going from one of my aunt's homes back to my house.

I like nights like this. There is a different silence; you can almost hear our Mother Earth 'E'tinohah- breathing softly in her sleep. Taking her rest from the busy seasons and getting ready for the next cycle. There was always a comfort in these kind of nights. A comfort that held you safe and silently told you "Everything is o.k."

We climb up on the shore and drive into Moose Factory. As we drive I remember some of the jokes I've heard about this place. This place where they make moose. In my mind I can see an assembly line and workers are attaching new antlers on a nearly finished moose.

"So, Joseph, this is where you guys make the moose huh?"

"Yeah right, just don't get on the part attaching the tails."

We both chuckle over this. I like this man, even though we only met two days ago. He moves with a deep sincerity and honesty that reminds me of my older uncles. His eyes show that he has seen a lot, and that he has struggled mightily not to give in to the craziness that comes from seeing things before you're 20 years old that no one should see in their whole lives.

Most Native eyes are like that. I imagine mine are like that. I see it in my 17-year-old daughter's eyes. By the time she was 15 she had been to 11 funerals, almost all of them family members or close friends. I wonder if there are any white 15 year olds who have seen as much death as her?

The houses here all look pretty much the same. Hooray for government housing. Southern homes in a northern environment, this really makes sense, huh?

We pull into the driveway of a one-storey ranch style house that could just as well be in the suburbs of Toronto or Hamilton. It's in need of painting, and maybe a couple of windows could be replaced- your typical, predictable "rez" house.

Helen greets us at the door and, after we remove our boots, guides us to the proverbial kitchen table. "The Table," where all form of business is conducted. "The Table," from which Native mothers, grandmothers and aunties have run the world throughout this century.

"This is my mother," Helen starts the introductions. "Mother, this is Mike, the one I told you about who is doing the workshop."

"Wahgiye," she says to us, and then says something else in Cree that I assume means, "Have a seat," since Joseph is easing himself into a chair after shaking hands with her. I shake her hand and take a seat next to her.

Helen asks, "Do you want coffee or tea?"

"Coffee, thanks" I reply. I remember there was a time when you visited the older folks and all you got was tea. Tea was the national drink of the old timers no matter which nation you visited.

As soon as we have been given our drinks Helen sits down opposite me and begins talking to her mother in Cree. "I'm telling my mother who you are, and why you have come to visit," she explains almost apologetically.

I want to say, "Don't apologize to me for your language. I'm the foreigner. If anything, I'm the one who should be apologizing for forcing English into this house." But I don't, instead I make a face and nod my head, hoping that she gets the non-verbal message - "No need to explain, it's o.k."

Her mother looks at me for what seems to be a long time, but in fact is probably only 15 seconds. Our older people have that way of looking that gives you the realization of what a microbe feels like under a microscope. There is an intensity in their eyes as they look you over, an intensity that you feel scan your insides.

The corners of her mouth turn up almost unperceptively, and she turns to her daughter and speaks for some time in Cree. Her voice has a quality to it that makes you feel like everything's going to be all right. I can imagine running to her with a cut finger, or a bump on the head, and that voice taking the hurt of the world away.

"My mother says she is glad you have come to visit. She says..." and for a split second there is a blush of embarrassment,"... you look like a good man. A man that works hard, and believes deeply in what he does."

Now it's my turn to be embarrassed. A discomfort arises out of the pit of my stomach and makes it way up my spine to the back of my neck. I've come to recognize this gesture I have with my head whenever I'm uncomfortable. I involuntarily give my head a quick, small twist that always seems to control the embarrassment.

"My mother says your face looks familiar, she thinks she has seen it on t.v.. Were you on t.v. for something?"

"During Oka I was one of the negotiators, and was on t.v. a couple of times. Maybe that's where she saw me."

At the mention of Oka during the translation her mother looked directly at me. There was a proud, happy glint in her eyes. When she spoke there was an excitement in her voice.

"My mother says she thought she had seen you before. She thinks it was during the time of Oka. She wants you to know she thinks your people are brave people. She was so happy to see someone stand up to the government. She watched it all the time, until the end."

Her mother spoke again for some time. This time her voice vacillated between a hint of anger and a hint of sadness. Neither feeling was expressed clearly, but you could hear their presence.

"My mother says that the government has done much to us Indians. Much that isn't good. She is glad that you younger ones are willing to fight back, and not let these things happen again."

As I listened, I thought to myself, "It's always nice to be called a 'younger one' when you're 44." As I looked at her I realized I couldn't tell her age. There are the wrinkles and gray hair, but something seems to shine through - something from her spirit that creates an image of agelessness.

"She says that she has seen much in her time. I've told her before what you said about the sterilization. She says she thought something was going wrong with all of the women, but couldn't understand what it was."

I looked at the mother and nodded. Then I asked Helen, "How old is your mother, and what's her name?"

Once again, Helen blushed, "I'm sorry, her name is Nelly and she will be 71 this year. She lived most of her life in the Bush. First with her family, then with my father. They didn't come to Moose Factory to live full time until the mid-sixties. They only came in because of our going to school, and the trapping was getting bad. If the government hadn't forced us into school we probably would have stayed in the Bush. I know she really misses that life, she talks about it all the time."

"How big is your family?"

"There are seven of us, four brothers and three sisters. Us first four were all born in the Bush, but the rest were born at the hospital here."

"Is your father still alive?"

"No, he died four years ago. Would you care for more coffee?" The tone in her voice said she didn't want to talk about her father.

Nelly began speaking again. No matter what the language, you can always hear the questioning, and it sounded like she had several of them.

"My mother wants to know what it's like where you come from? Do you have the same problems with the government? Do your people still speak their language, keep their culture?"

"I come from the south. My home rez is in western New York. We have 18 communities of Iroquois people in Quebec, Ontario, New York, and out west in Wisconsin and Oklahoma.

We're doing our best to try and keep our languages going. It's a tough fight but some of our people have come up with some good approaches. It's the same with the culture. A lot more of our people are trying to follow their own ways. There are lots of young people coming back to the traditions."

Helen translates all of this to her mother. As Helen speaks Nelly nods her head. Nelly stares into her tea cup as she listens. Her eyes focus so intently, so deeply I get the impression she sees something in the tea. I remember as a child my grandmother taking me to Hattie's, our local person who reads the leaves. That was the same look I remember Hattie having.

This time when Nelly speaks she goes on for quite awhile. Her hands fondle the cup, and every once in a while she looks up. When she looks up it doesn't seem to be for any reason to look at anything in the room. Instead, her eyes look beyond the room, as though she were looking into another realm, another place.

Whatever Nelly has said seems to have gotten to Helen. Her translation starts in a slow, low voice. Her hands fidget with her cup.

"My mother was just talking about some of the changes she has seen." She begins, "She was telling about how nice it used to be. How people got along together, and helped each other. She says that has changed so much."

"She says the biggest change she has seen is that there is so much death now, and so much sadness because of it."

Helen's eyes begin to take on the same far away look as her mother's.

"What really hurts her is that there are so many young ones dying. She says she can't figure out why this is happening, but it is and it hurts our people so much."

Nelly begins talking again, her hands still cradling her cup, her eyes still looking at that other place. Helen is obviously having to control her feelings, she is swallowing several times and her concentration is locked on to a pattern in the table cloth. Joseph shifts uncomfortably in his chair. He inhales very deeply on his cigarette and gives you the impression he would much rather be somewhere else.

I've gone into my 'listening mode.' Over the years I've listened to so many heart-breaking stories I've developed this ability to close down my emotional side. There's a coldness that my head feels like a radar unit. My eyes and ears pick up every nuance, the slightest gesture. My concentration locks on to the speaker.

Tonight my 'radar' has locked onto all three people. Nelly has locked her feelings away so she can recount this story. Her story is stirring up a sadness within Helen, and restlessness that seems to be linked to anger in Joseph.

"My mother says she knows the residential school had something to do with these problems."

Her voice shifts my attention from the room to her. "She says she saw the changes in all of us children when we came back from there."

"She says she always felt the hurt inside of us but didn't know how to help us. All she could do was pray and try to be extra nice to us, but she could always feel the hurt."

"She talked about how lonely she got when we were away, and how she worried about us." Helen's voice is strained she is using all her control to keep her feelings in check.

"She says there were times when she would dream about us, and sometimes she saw us being hurt in those dreams. She said all she could do was pray that her dream weren't true."

As I listen I stare at Helen's hands. I'm suddenly aware of how intense my concentration is, this story is starting to get to me. I pull in a deep breath through my nose and the feeling subsides.

"She says that while we were away things were happening to her. She is talking about something that happened to her at the hospital." At this point Helen lights up a cigarette and inhales deeply. Joseph gets up and pours more coffee for me and him.

As Nelly continues to talk I am aware that there is a different coldness rising in my chest. I recognize this one too. It's the cold anger that often comes when I hear stories like this.

Nelly's voice has changed ever so slightly. She can't keep the sadness out any longer. Her hands lie on each side of the cup now, motionless. Her shoulders have dropped ever so slightly.

Everyone else in the room has picked up on this change. Helen's eyes are on her mother and are filled with tears that won't flow. Joseph lights another cigarette off the butt of the last one, and then crushes out the old one

Helen's voice sounds controlled when she starts to talk, but her eyes still have tears that won't flow. "My mother went to hospital to deliver her last three children. She says the three times she went in they started giving her some kind of pills to take. She says they told her the pills were to help her with having children. She says from the time she started taking those pills she felt different inside. She said each time she got pregnant she said the children felt different inside of her. For a long time she couldn't understand what was going on."

"She says during her last pregnancy she had some dreams in which she saw her baby struggling with something. She couldn't tell what that thing was, but when she woke up she realized it was the pill they were giving her."

"She says about four or five years after her last child she heard that the hospital had been experimenting on the Indian women here. She heard they had been given a pill called thalidomide, and that this pill hurt the babies. She wants to know if you know anything about this?"

I'm caught off guard by the question. I've been concentrating on listening and holding off the cold anger. The anger began to grow stronger as I envisioned this naive, trusting woman being taken advantage of by these doctors and nurses.

I look at Nelly and tell Helen, "Yes, I know about the drug, but I don't know about them giving the pill out up here. The drug proved to be a huge problem because it caused a lot of birth defects. The pill did a lot of damage."

As Helen translates I pick a spot on the opposite wall to focus in on. It feels as though I can send this cold anger out through my forehead and embed it into the wall.

Nelly is talking again. The sadness sounds stronger. The corners of her eyes seem to sag and you can feel the weight that rests on her shoulders. This is the sight that pushes up the anger in me. It must cause the same reaction in Joseph because I feel the same coldness coming from him.

"My mother says she believes this pill has caused problems in two of my brothers and one sister. None of them have been able to have children."

A bitterness is beginning to form in Helen's voice. It's a bitterness that begins when one's trust has been betrayed. These people have trusted these hospitals and the people who work there. Yes, they have had their suspicions, but the bottom line is that they trusted them.

"Helen, has your mother ever talked about this before?" I ask.

"No, this is the first she has said of this to me. We have never talked about these things before." The tears have gone from her eyes, she has managed to pull them back into her body.

The room is quiet for a few moments. Helen is the first to react. She almost snatches a cigarette out of the pack. Her mouth is firm as she lights it, deeply inhales and says, "Can you see what they have done to my family? They have stopped us from having children, they have stopped us from having a full future."

She takes a deep swallow from her tea. "I'm so mad, I don't know what to do."

Joseph is leaning forward on one elbow, the other on his knee. He says, "When I was at St. Anne's the priests did a lot of things to me and the others. I used to lie in my bed thinking about home. I had all these wonderful pictures in mind how nice it would be to get back home."

You can almost hear the wistful little boy in his voice as he speaks. His eyes are flashing back and forth between two deep feelings. In one second the eyes search for that time of peace and safety in his grandmother's lap. In the next second his eyes are telling me that he would like to find the ones who did this to his grandmother and make them pay.

I know this struggle well; I've gone through it myself. His eyes narrow, and you feel the anger coming out of them. His shoulders are stiff and straight from controlling the urge to shake and vibrate from the hurt welling up inside. When he speaks it's from between tight jaws, and emotional control to not let the venom get into the words.

"What she is telling you is only part of what has happened to us up here. What she said in Cree is much more, it's hard to translate it all. If you could hear it all you would be deeply affected."

"Joseph, I am deeply affected. Nelly's story hits me as much as any story I have heard anywhere else. Right now I have a ball in my stomach from the anger I feel. The point is, what do you want to do about it?"

He looks me straight in the eyes. "Honestly?" he asks.

I nod my head 'yes,' even though I already know the answer.

"I'd like to shoot someone," he rasps out through that cold anger that could turn hot in a split second. It is the same answer I have heard all over the continent.

Helen is looking at Joseph with a concern in her eyes. She believes he is capable of doing it. You can hear the panic in her voice when she asks, "What would that prove? You're the one who would end up in jail, then what would happen to your family?"

"Helen, Joseph said he feels that way, not that he would do it. Quite honestly, I feel the same way. A lot of times that feeling gets real big inside of me. When it happens I have to go and get some help to unload it or it feels like I'll go over the edge." I say this to calm her panic because I've seen this reaction before.

Our women hold a long memory of all of the men who have been killed. There is still a lot of grief that has not been let go over all those who have been slaughtered. We don't need to argue right now about what we would like to do - we need the unfettered ability to express whatever we need to express because it is all valid.

All three are looking at me. Helen has a questioning look on her face. Joseph has a look of recognition that says, "Here's someone who knows how I feel." Nelly is looking inside me again; she is the one I want to talk to at this moment.

As I look directly into her eyes my insides fill up with a warmth that spreads out from just above my stomach outward into my arms and legs, and then into my head, filling my eyes with the huge love and caring I have for this woman.

"Helen, could you translate what I say as close as possible?"

She nods her head.

As I look at Nelly I see my grandmother, my aunties, and all those other beautiful Native ladies who have had to endure so much all these years. Their endurance has kept us alive in so many ways. Who I am today as a Native man is because of them. The fact that my children will have a culture to inherit is because of them.

"Grandmother, I am so sorry that so much has happened to you that has taken away some of the happiness that you deserve. I want to take this opportunity to share with you some words that were given to our people to help us with the heavy feelings that can come over us."

"If I had it in me I would take the softest of deer hide and wipe your eyes. During the time of this hurt our eyes fill with tears and we can't see the Creation or our loved ones very well. With this soft hide we would remove those tears so you could see the Creation and all of its beauty, and see the loved ones who are still here and care for you so much."

As Helen translates Nelly looks up and the corners of her mouth turn up ever so slightly. A small gleam returns to her eyes.

"If I had it with me I would take the softest down from an eagle and use it to clear your ears. During the time of our hurt our ears have become blocked by the sound of our crying from inside. When it is this way we can't hear the beautiful sound of the Creation, or our loved ones as they express their caring for us."

With this translation Nelly's face begins to warm, a fuller smile returns and her eyes hold a look of hope. This is what our people need most times, words of encouragement and acknowledgement of the grief and hurt they have been carrying.

"We have been told that water is a sweet medicine. We use this medicine to remove the blockage we have felt in our throat, and to remove the sour feeling we have in our stomach. During the time of our grief and hurt we have been unable to speak the words we really want to say to the Creation and our loved ones. It is the grief and hurt that creates that sick feeling in our stomachs. The gift of water is that it helps to remove these things and restore the fire within us that is our spirit."

All three have begun to relax. The tension has left Helen's voice as she translates. Joseph is paying close attention to the words. Nelly is looking more energized.

"Tell your mother that during the rest of the workshop we will be discussing what can be done about these kind of situations. I do not believe or accept the notion that these things should be allowed to lie quietly. We were created to be powerful, wonderful humans, not oppressed and hurt people."

"We can achieve healing, but we have to do it on our terms, in our way. The ones who oppress us can't find their way out of this. It is up to us to come up with the process that will produce real healing in our world."

Nelly speaks to Helen for a long time. Her voice holds the sound of remembering, you can see her mind reaching back and bringing forth something she hasn't talked about in some time.

"My mother wants you to know that she deeply appreciates the words you shared with us. She says these words remind her of things she heard when she was a little girl. She says she remembers the old people speaking like that. She says these are the words and acts of kindness we must bring back to each other.

"She says that if these are the words that are in your heart and mind then you will always do good work for the people."

I look at the clock and it's now 11:50. "Helen, it's getting late and we need to get ready for tomorrow. Tell your mother I've enjoyed meeting her and being here. I want to come over again before I leave."

Helen translates this to her mother who looks up at me and smiles. She nods her head and speaks for a moment.

"My mother would be glad to have you come over again. She said to come for supper. It's not right that we didn't feed you well on this visit." Helen appears somewhat embarrassed at this final part.

Joseph and I rise from our chairs, shake hands with Nelly and prepare to leave. At the door Helen stops me. "I want to thank you for coming over. My mother and I have a lot to talk about. I'm beginning to understand some things about her I didn't before. I haven't always shown my love to her and it's time we healed that. Thank you."

I can't say anything, the embarrassment is creeping back up my neck. So I just smile and nod my head in understanding.

Outside it is still that peaceful kind of cold night. Joseph and I stop to light up before getting into the truck. In my mind a thought jumps into my consciousness, "After the freezing comes the thaw. With the thaw comes the renewal of life. Our E'tinohah and all the females are responsible for this. We, the males, have to guard and insure that this cycle continues. No more lost futures!"

I look at Joseph: "No more lost futures, Joseph. We don't take this shit no more."

His face breaks into a huge smile: "That's right, no more lost futures."

The ride back still has that bungee-jumping quality to it, just waiting for the loud cracking sound of the ice beginning to give way and we got to make a run for it. Life is a rush sometimes and I really savour those moments.

LAST RITES

I stop the clocks in the house cover mirrors with sorry
purple cloth
eating hard boiled I sit on furniture bare of its cushions
telling the four corners of your life on earth
what do I know of your living? you were always home
for me
to listen to argue me to stay in this town I'd say doesn't
fit you can't take it back you'd say
I would always laugh knowing it meant you really just
wanted me to stay

your body should have been washed in the finest herbs
and flowers then wrapped in soft cloth
instead they slit you open like a fish inspected you like
so many sides of beef left you ripe
bleeding the blood where they would find the drugs they
say took you into the next world
you should have been body painted blue you should
have been given a special tatoo so your ancestors would
recognize you
those hunters and gatherers you were so proud of would
call you back let you inside the special red door

fashioning you a new age tombstone your new car and
the fence in front of it
I put up a bouquet of freesias calla lilies and birds of
paradise
your pictures hanging from colored ribbons flutter free
on the chain link
soon other friend's gifts appear candles crystal bowls
full of water and chocolate
no grave site more befitting the parking lot of the city
where your spirit still saturates

in three short days my offerings like your body become
ashes swimming in a black night
while our drums beat you a warrior's farewell sage
wafting our prayers up to the turquoise sky
your last wish of me granted I am here planted not
remembering where or why I was going away

THE STRANGER

stumbling through the darkened streets one night
i chanced upon an image. it blocked my way
so in way of being polite, i asked it what it was doing.
fine, it said, which i thought was strange
because this did not answer my question
and tears were running from its eyes
so i knew that it was lying.
i stared longingly for a moment.
but once recognized, i knew that this was just a gimmick.
i quickly averted mine own eyes
and tried to make in haste my depart
but stumbling over my own feet
i landed in the gutter.
this stranger helped me up and said
i'm sorry i startled you, but having known you,
for a very long time, wonder why you still ignore me.
just admit that you know me
and i will gladly not disturb you,
but until that time, when you and i can walk
with pride, i will never leave you.

Jennifer Tsun

MAYBE TOMORROW

I was out gathering willow
to make baskets
at the edge of the frozen swamp
the sky was very blue
the air was aching full of quietness
I was feeling happy
having left my cares and worries
where they fell on the snowside

suddenly
a pair of chickadees
lighted in the branches
near to me
chattering in chickadee language
one hopped closer to me
so very close
fluffing up his chest
looking into my eye
with his little black button eye
talking so seriously to me
of very important things:

how I longed to
understand

maybe some day
if I listen very well
I will
just like in days
of long ago
some day
very soon
maybe
tomorrow

NA'AH*

She is afraid to sleep at night
for she can see the light;
"WHY DO YOU LIVE UP HERE?"
They call to her.
Husbands and friends
who walked into the light
enchanted by the sight;
"COME WITH US..."
they sing
holding onto the angel's wing
trying so hard
to step past her guard.
"NAY**"
She tells them
holding the key
that could set her soul free.

*Na'ah means "grandmother" in Gitskan
**Nay means "no" in Gitskan

ROSEANNE

1

Silence.
The proud flicker of distant wings.
Poised
To carve a world he stands alone
Before the wind's soft murmur
Of patience extending to the world's rim.
Quiet moments, stones in the midst of streams.
Seconds of watching the steam rise from coffee cups
In early morning stillness.
To need the use of a million words
For a single song of joy.
The scratchings of a pen at 2 a.m.
When the only witness to the Caesarian birth of an idea
Are the green eyes of an alley cat who sits
On the window ledge
Looking on with the indifference of a tree.
Cruel moments when the germinal of a song
Is frozen by the memory of a smile
Or the quiet closing of a closet door.

2

Out of my surroundings I created myself. At midnight I extended the darkness; perhaps from behind one of the shadowed trees which lined the path would step my Fate. I waited but nothing happened so I continued walking, stumbling once in crossing a low man-made ditch. I stumbled again, this time over a thinly concealed branch, before I found myself that cold night on the edge of the forest near a large open field.

It lay there, a vacant lot, an eye socket emptied
while rain fell in drizzles. The night
grew colder and a breeze stirred from somewhere
beyond loosened wires no longer barriers.
There was no protest as the first snowflake
burnt to the field and was devoured;
nor was there protest as another
followed the path of the first.
After, there was a hush of many minutes,
a breathing pause as the field
sank deeper into the dark, a gathering pause
while the sky sank deeper into grey.
The light started from everywhere
as the field loosened its grip on identity.
From somewhere beyond the mountain's rim,
from somewhere beyond granite shoulders,
stirred light emerged to colour the sky,
but not sight.

3

Beaten roads lead the way
To a new sun, a beach smoothly sanded
Beneath the sparrowed heavens.
Episode Two of a drained story
Leaves us on the shores of the writer's world
Having to twist the sea's rhythm to suit our own.
We have drummed into our souls the music
From another world. More's the shame
That we've learned as well to dance with it.
Our singers are locked in day's brightness
Away from our shadow worlds; there is no shelter
From the storm. You and I do not belong.
We have no words of our own for hope
Because hope then had no meaning; Faith was all
Until we learned despair; trust was all
Until we learned violence. If the world
Spins to a new day it has left us behind,
Washed ashore by cold dark waves.

4

Eyes gleam from taut erect bodies
straining upwards, waiting for the sun.
In the flickering light of the fire
I dance
although even this merges into shadow.
The movements are correct;
I can dance with the best.
but it is not there, the spirit is gone.
The old people smile and nod and moan;
I have fooled them but the fire is not fooled.
Twisted shadows on forest walls
mockingly shift with my feet.
As the tale unfolds I shift, the world shifts;
the strong pulse of the earth flows in my veins.
The last part of the tale
unfolds in the twilight hours
and in the twilight hours
I dance alone.

5

I've seen the tears in your eyes
Turn your heart into one of stone.
And I've waited in silence to the feeling
That your troubles will remain unknown.
And I've wanted to say so strongly
To you that I love you.
But the words won't come and your tears
Continue in silence as I sit next to you.
I cannot share your laughter
So how can I understand your tears?
I've sat for hours waiting for your words
But the cliff is still there in your eyes.

6

She walks in shadows which follow her
On the brightest days of the year.
Her words are those of someone who isn't there
But somewhere beyond the fields where we sit.
Her paths are twisted by the dreams
Of fragmented realities beyond her reach.
I have watched the shadows flicker over her soul
But I can only turn the other way when her eyes
Search mine for common feelings.
Single-handedly she would redefine
The role of poetry in our world,
Although I have told her that the drift and sway
Of her inner visions are not those
The world would care to hear.
And often when her heart would falter
She would reach out in search of my support
But I could not comfort her
For I was not in touch with my own visions.

Her epitaph is one she has written herself
And the shadows she struggles against are hers alone.

7

The scratchings of a pen
Pushing stories beyond the night's darkness;
The green cat eyes of boredom gazing
Into the room from the unseen windowsill.
The deliberate refrain from writing in order
To build a single chord into a symphony of motion;
The measured eyes of those more certain of themselves
Than any poem I can construct.
Coffee stains and the well-worn phrase;
The recurrent hiss of passing traffic;
These and other reveries disturb early-morning dreams.
Written lines have their own minds;
Dilettante explorers quickly jot memories.
After the rain has washed the earth
The robin returned this morning
And the waves
Wiped clean the silent beaches.
Clean, too, the streets reflecting last night's concerns.
New puddles cast old reflections-
No different perspective, only
The new form of Age.

8

Satisfied, he sighed,
Let the sun extend into skin.
Shaped by trees, hands
Curled about the wood staff.
Eyes pierced leaf patterns
To the beaten path's grey dust.
Quiet heat
Shimmered above the lake.
Sounds of distant voices
Extended beyond hearing into memory.
Floating eagle's wings have no motion.
Footfalls on damp forest floors
Are recalled, with the sun
Blazing through tree walls.
Lift a hand and the forest stops.
A leaf falls.
        Hands quiver.
Limbs shake.
        Small paws
Scream across the glade.

9

Sunlight throws its beaded patterns into a roomful
of memories, lights upon the picture which now
I can gaze at without the sharp sense of pain
it once brought to me, the thoughts of a woman
too soon placed beyond my reach, a woman
who now lies beneath the cross's grey shadows.
Her death has left me with only the memories
of a winter scene where her breath misted into fog,
a quiet morning moment when she sat alone
cradling a scalding cup of coffee
between fragile hands weakened by fatigue;
a moment when, not knowing I was present,
she wept at the death of her friend
in the fading glow of her own life.
Listening to the drift of the music
has touched chords within myself which I thought
were gone forever, which I thought were completed
in a six-year dream of my own creation.
I've moved beyond that now and can only pray
that her memories will not wear with age
like the whisper of soft rain upon the deserted graveyard.

10

Aged litanies etched in stone
with word to word - meanings have grown.
Stirred singing, leaved rustling-
downing trails I went my way.
Snowing field and colder biting,
more than this I will not say.

SLEEPWALKER

The PLASTIC lamination curdled,
black smoke stinking

        choking

and my see-through stare
        blessed the FLAMES

as my status card burned

as my STATUS card burned

imnotyourindiananymore
im not your indian anymore

I'm not your Indian anymore

I'M NOT YOUR INDIAN ANYMORE

        no more.

Chris Bose

ALCOHOLISM
FRONT LINE BATTLES

Fortunately or otherwise, I can remember painfully, clearly, the very first bottle of liquor I bought and consumed. It was what my "friends" and I called a "Mickey". It was, I believe, a three hundred fifty millilitre bottle of, "Smirnoff" vodka, or poison if you will. I drank it straight, no mix, no chaser, in one rough, blurry night.

I don't remember the exact date, I believe it was in the spring of nineteen eighty-five, and for sure I don't remember what happened that fateful night. But that was the start of a long journey to reality and finding out who I am and what I am doing in life, my purpose. I'm not really sure if I want to know what happened during that dark, tragic night so long ago, in my dim warehouse called a memory.

The "blackout" I had the first time I got drunk was like the starting point of many more to come. I thought the darkness was home.

That night still affects me. I still think about it. I still ask myself why I did it, and the effects will live with me forever. The effects of this self-abuse still leave me feeling the repercussions of my drinking days and daze. At first I hid the bottle, then I hid from everything, and ran from everything. I became a quitter. I even ran from myself.

Each time I had a drink, I would drink to get completely drunk; I had no stopping point. I would go until the liquor was gone. Each time I did, I would lose myself a little more. My self-esteem and self-respect would get crushed by the bottle. I would be the jester, the fool, but in reality I felt as though I was drinking broken glass and lemon juice. I bled on the inside, letting my self-worth drain from my body, tears to blood. Each time becoming a different person, continually running from the mirror in my mind, not wanting to deal with it, not wanting to look in it.

The loss of my self-esteem, self-respect and pride made me insecure, which filled me with jealously and envy of others whose lives looked better, clearer, and those who had more direction. This brought me to what we all learn, a creature called "Hatred."

I lashed out at everyone and anything. I became violent and had an extremely low tolerance point for anything - it didn't take much to anger me. If I felt that something or anyone was superior in any way I would put all my insecurities to work and find something to hate about it. Eventually this was not just when I was drinking; I soon became like this all the time.

All that anger and hate soon led to fighting and violence, quite quickly actually. I fought with everyone, my close friends, my family, my girlfriend. Anyone I felt threatened by, I would unleash my repressed emotions. Sometimes it was actual physical fighting and other times it was verbal or emotional abuse. Almost always these fights were really about petty things. My view of reality was fairly twisted and distorted. I just needed something or someone to take my own damn insecurities out on, I was so damn blind.

When reality becomes distorted like that, a person becomes oblivious to their surroundings. Nothing else matters but the bottle. I ran so far and chased everyone away and soon I just found the only one there was, the bottle. It's sad that when you think that you're really alone and that no one cares, it isn't that way. It's just you've temporarily chased everyone away. Huge amounts of money were getting spent in this stage. Days began to blur and only "Partying" really seemed to matter. This is the dangerous zone because if something doesn't happen quickly in this stage this is where life long habits can be formed.

Something did happen to me in this stage of alcoholism. I awoke one day at approximately 5:23 in the morning in the hospital here in town. I had been involved in a fight. I remember thinking I was dead, because all I saw when I opened my eyes was light. I have never been so scared in my life. It was then I finally looked in the mirror and saw a beaten, bloody punching bag. And through that I saw who I was, and realized what I was running after couldn't be found in alcohol, for in that there was only death. What I finally realized was that I couldn't run from my problems anymore. It doesn't solve anything, the problems just become compounded and grow and grow. I was tired of running and I had nowhere else to run to, so after seven years of abuse I finally laid to rest the bottle.

It's been two years and I don't even think about drinking anymore. I quit stone cold. That morning in the hospital did it for me. I finally saw who I had become in the mirror. I know I never will, as long as I live, be that hideous creature again.

i am your grandson

grandfather, i have come to speak,
to listen to you.

i have come to say
i am your grandson,
and i can hear your song
sung on the stormy shore.

like the salt from the sea spray,
i can taste the spirit
of your life.

you died long ago
in sorrow, as
your son's spirit was
splintered like cedar.

i stand
facing the wind and waves.

i stand here
i am your grandson.

my voice is weak,
sing through my throat.

Frank Conibear

i have come to say
that
i am your grandson,
that i have come to listen.
i ask for strength
of your spirit
so i can face this day.

give me strength
i am your grandson.

hiatch ka siyam,

thank you

grandfather.

PROTECT THE ISLAND

Across the mid-summer sun
an aluminium boat.
Suddenly aware
I watch it approach
measure distance
in the blink of an eye.

Lifted from a solitude of loons.
I stand.
Protect the island.
It's a lifesaver.
You can't take it with you.
It's a breath of fresh air.

Six vacationers land,
slurring themselves.
Whiskey walk.
I approach. My lungs full and tense.
They call: Where are the fish?
I reply: In the north channel, but they're belly-up.
the rain is vinegar.

Cursing
they say they will write Washington
and Ottawa
and it won't be love letters.
They salute
pile into the boat and shove off.
At the shore trees bow
in the recent wind
offering the greatest applause.

ON THE VERGE OF A DREAM AND EXPLOITATION

When she walks, she walks
carrying a large eye as a suitcase,
it helps her keep the dreams in focus.

Baby, she wants it all, she can see it.
It's all right there for her big eye to see.
She wants a car
She wants a man
She wants a home
She wants it all...

Tyrone thinks its all bull: Her little dreams won't get her too far: She's got looks - But that's all; Tyrone thinks it all bull; he waits and he thinks.

She dreams of having it all. When she walks, she walks from the streets of Placid City to the junction of Dreams and Exploitation. Through the multitudes of men, she can only think of one. When she undresses, he's there watching her, making love to her, his wings and business suit never felt so good.

Tyrone checks his time
-Damn woman
-Off in Dreamland again
-Don't she know I've got a business to run
-I's not gonna be a janitor forever
-That's for damn sure

She puts her black knitted dress back over her shoulders, closes her purse and dreams of skiing at Showboat Springs. She's never been there except thru the pages of a magazine. She lives at the Algonquin Hotel on Double Trouble where the ripped up pages of magazines line the street.

Tyrone don't like that bellhop there,
that man's black hair and braids bother him,
He must be doing time with his girl.
She's talking her bull again
How she wants a boy with a war bonnet

War Bonnet?
Get Real
Dis is da Goaden age Baby
My dreams are your dreams

And we exploit together

Dorothy Christian

"A PLANE RIDE TO THE FUTURE"

Jeanne laid in bed in total darkness, wide awake -- Waiting for him to return. As the clock slowly and agonizing guided the minute hand around and around, she went over and over the day's events... trying to understand.

Today is Valentine's Day -- weren't men and women who were together as couples supposed to at least pretend to be loving towards each other? The T.V. commercials and magazine adverts presented such a romantic picture of this day set aside to honour the love between couples. Jeanne did not see any roses or any chocolates on her table but then she should know better, the people in those ads were always rich looking, white people.

Jeanne's Valentine's Day was a whole other reality. Why did he shut her out with the silent treatment when she came home from work? Why was he drinking? Why did he leave when she asked him to explain his behaviour? He knew she was busy preparing to go to Vancouver on a business trip and could not take the afternoon off like he wanted her to. He knew Jeanne had to pack and get all the last minute things done. He knew Jeanne would see her family when she was in the west. He seemed to be threatened by her family. Jeanne was not going to put him ahead of her family or her work... not any more. At least she didn't think so. Jeanne was still confused by what happened on Tuesday.

She got up to have a cigarette... and another and then another. Chainsmoking did not give Jeanne insight into what was happening in her life; nor did the nicotine bring understanding, only more fear and anxiety. She started trembling inside and out, just remembering....

Three days earlier, Jeanne and Doug had invited her ex-roommate over for dinner. Susan was into gourmet cooking and she sparkled as fragrances of her salad, main course, and dessert filled the apartment. Susan knew her talents and confidently displayed them when she could. After the dessert and coffee, everyone went into the living room. By now, Susan and Doug had consumed at least two bottles of wine. Jeanne had one glass of wine. She was purposefully reserved in her alcohol intake because she was working on eliminating alcohol from her body and her life. She knew the destruction it had wreaked on her family and community.

From the bathroom, Jeanne could smell the aroma of marijuana. Oh no, they were smoking up too. Reluctantly, she moved towards the living room. Could she ask them to stop? She had let it go too far already. She should never have allowed the wine. What now? Oh, the hell with it, she may as well join them. Jeanne did not want to argue with anyone. The pot would just make her sleep anyway. She never did understand why people liked the stuff... all it did for her was make her foggy in her thinking and seeing.

When she got back to the living room Jeanne could see very clearly what was happening. Susan was sitting very provocatively in front of Doug. The top two buttons on her blouse were opened suggesting that the mysteries of her body wanted to be opened too. Doug was obviously consumed in the possibilities. Rashly Jeanne puffed on the joint in short, intense drags and poured herself another glass of wine. Maybe, just maybe she could create the right amount of haze to kill the pain she felt at the pit of her stomach.

Her stomach wrenched as she openly challenged Susan and Doug. She knew Susan was a frustrated white woman, who was fast approaching her mid-forties and was desperately hanging onto whatever youth she had. She was in between relationships and right now, anyone would do--- even someone else's man, someone else's Indian man. Maybe Susan still figured she was an Olympic runner - still pursuing that gold metal she didn't get at the Olympics! Jeanne had pondered Doug's fascination with white women, and was specifically observing his momentary fascination with Susan. It made her think of all the racist comments he had made about how he would never be caught dead with a white woman and how they were only good for one thing. She remembered hearing the confusion and the anger in his voice when he spoke of his ex-wife who happened to be a white woman. Jeanne did not understand the complexities of why Indian men were captivated by white women but she knew she was witnessing the dynamics of it right at this very moment. "Hey you two, should I make a pot of coffee? I must tell you both I am not into threesomes or menage a trois or whatever they call them", said Jeanne very pointedly, with just a slight edge of sarcasm, as she moved to the kitchen.

Jeanne had learned the white man's directness very well and sometimes people called her brutally honest. In time she would learn the indirectness of her own people was a more valuable communication tool. At least a person is left with their dignity when communicating

Indian style. One thing she knew for sure -- there was no dignity in what was happening in the living room.

She went to the kitchen and put the coffee on and quietly went to her bedroom. Jeanne carefully gathered her abalone shell and her sage. There was a peacefulness emanating from her sacred things. Somewhere deep within her she knew she was not to handle these sacred things when she was indulging in alcohol and pot. But somehow Jeanne knew the Creator would understand and forgive her this indiscretion. It felt absolutely necessary for her to burn this sage right now. She felt an urgent need for a sense of strength and the burning smoke of sage invariably gave her that strength. As she lowered her head to the shell to collect the burning smoke over her head, Doug burst into the bedroom.

He was cursing and swearing and started punching and kicking her. He was yelling, "What the hell do you think you're doing? Since when do you tell me anything? You never tell me what to do, do you understand that? You never interrupt me, do you understand?". Jeanne was trying to protect her head as he swung at her --- Susan came rushing into the bedroom and wrestled herself between Jeanne and Doug. Somehow Susan pulled Doug away from Jeanne and he seemed to calm down. Jeanne could see the fear and horror in Susan's blue eyes. Inside herself, Jeanne stomach churned, flip flopped and knotted into a huge ball. Cautiously all three of them moved away from each other. Susan pulled herself together and immediately left without so much as a backward glance. She even left her cookware. Jeanne wondered if privileged white women ever had to deal with this kind of violent situations in their relationships. She knew that Indian women had to deal with it and some chose to live with it as much as they abhorred it!

Jeanne was still trying to understand what had happened in her bedroom three days ago...

Jeanne could hear his key turning in the keyhole. No, it wasn't turning. Quickly she put out her cigarette and went down the stairs, she could still hear what sounded like his key. Slowly she opened the door to a totally pitiful sight. There was Doug, so drunk he couldn't stand, he was on his knees trying to fit the key into the keyhole. His coat was recklessly open and he boldly smiled at her as if to say, "Don't you dare say anything". As they climbed the stairs to the living room, she propped him up -- one arm behind him so he would not fall back down the stairs and one arm guiding him forward. The flight of stairs seemed endless.

In the living room, Doug kicked off his one snow boot. Obviously he had lost the other one and of course he didn't care --- most likely, he wasn't even aware of his loss. Jeanne sat on the couch not knowing what to do or what to expect. She had never seen Doug in this state before. In the three months of their relationship, Jeanne had seen Doug drink and smoke marijuana twice and both times he was not falling down drunk like he was now.

Internally she recoiled from him ... he brought back all the ugly memories of her childhood. Memories she had consciously worked on leaving behind, years ago. Jeanne thought if she acted lovingly towards him and helped him to bed, he would pass out-- just like they used to. She got up to help him take his coat off and suddenly there was a loud explosion.

Minutes, hours seemed to pass before Jeanne realized where the explosion came from, Doug had smashed the side of her head. Her left ear took the full weight of his blow and all she could hear was this loud thudding sound and a ringing somewhere in the distance. She did not know what was happening. Jeanne could hear this voice screaming and screaming -- somewhere in the middle of this huge black hole, this compelling familiar voice was calling for help. At some level, she wanted to respond to this voice but she knew right now she had to focus all her attention on fighting for her life. This man was going to kill her. He pulled handfuls of her hair out of her head. She could hear the strands of hair ripping from her scalp. His fist cracked against her head repeatedly. For an eternity, the ripping and cracking sounds reverberated through every fibre of Jeanne's being. He tore at her housecoat and ripped it to shreds. She was naked in the middle of her living room fighting off the kicks and punches to her stomach, her legs, her back, her shoulders. He didn't touch her face. The voice in the black hole kept shouting and wailing, getting louder and louder. Somewhere there was a sound... a knocking at the door.

The voice called from behind the front door, "This is the Police, what's going on up there? Are you alright? Your neighbours called-- they said they were afraid for your safety. Should we come up there?".

Jeanne pulled herself up from the middle of the living room floor and crawled to the hall closet to find something to cover her bruised naked body. Her arms were trembling as she slipped on her winter coat. And her fingers were so shaky she could hardly light a cigarette before going down the stairs.

Her voice quivered as she opened the door, "Yes, officer I think you should come up. This man has just tried to kill me". The policeman came up the stairs and saw Doug pulling his one snow boot on. "Does this man live here?", he asked. Jeanne could not believe the policemen would not just take Doug away. After many questions, they insisted this was his address too and they did not want to interfere in a domestic dispute. It was as if Jeanne was being punished. She had to go through what seemed like hours of agony in laying assault charges against Doug before the policemen would take him away.

Finally, they were all gone. Jeanne felt as if she had been beaten twice -- physically by Doug and emotionally and psychologically by the policemen. The policemen were so callous towards her. They made her feel as if this were her fault. Yet they were understanding and sympathetic towards Doug. They expected her to answer their questions in a rational way when the last thing in the world she felt was logical.

Jeanne had just lived through the most devastating, horrific, and terrorizing experience of her life. She fought for her life with every ounce of energy she had and they wanted her to be balanced and clear headed! How could they ever know the feeling of aloneness, beyond any depth of loneliness in that blackness that surrounds you ? How could they ever know the blackness of death as it envelops you? How could they ever know that? How could they ever know the feeling of your humanness being defiled?

All she wanted was a shower-- hot, hot water to caress her body and take away the jarring and humiliating effects of Doug's blows. She wanted to wash away this man from her life. She wanted to wash away forever, any smell or physical presence of him. Slowly and carefully Jeanne dried her body. First her arms, then her torso, then her legs. It was so important to be gentle...

She laid curled up in a fetal position sobbing and sobbing. The tears would not stop... they poured out of her, involuntarily. The muscles of her body ached, the thoughts of her mind raced, and her spirit yearned for love. Somehow she remembered her grandmother... her grandmother was love. Her grandmother's arms comforted her. Jeanne could hear her grandmother's voice, quietly and softly speaking to her.

Slowly she got up and went to her desk. She fumbled through the drawers and found some paper and a pen. She wrote: "Dear Doug: I am not sure what happened tonite or what caused it but it can never happen again. I want you out of my home and out of my life by the time I get back from Vancouver. I do not know what kind of upbringing you had and quite honestly I don't care right now. All I know is that I can't have you or anyone like you in my life. My grandmother brought me up believing and knowing about love between people, about tender, loving and caring. What happened tonite was not love but a pure expression of hatred and death. I touched death tonite and I know it was at your hands. Never again will this be allowed in my life. I have to continue to believe in what my grandmother taught me of love and humanity. And, I certainly cannot do that with you.

You need help and I hope for your sake that you get it. Good-bye."

Jeanne

Slowly Jeanne folded her letter and put it into an envelope. She attached it to the front door of the fridge, a conspicuous location so he could not claim he did not see it.

Jeanne felt comforted by the presence of her grandmother and she was able to return to her bedroom. Slowly and gently she unwrapped her abalone shell and sage from the red cotton cloth she protected them in. She flinched as she remembered how three nights ago, they had landed in the corner of the bedroom floor when Doug had attacked her during Susan's visit. She carefully lit the sacred medicine and felt the spiralling wisps of smoking sage envelope her body, mind, and spirit. Jeanne prayed for strength to get through this hideous event in her life. She was still visibly shivering but somehow the sage smoke made her stronger.

Jeanne could not sleep, her mind raced with a million thoughts of why Indian women tolerated men like Doug in their lives. Why did Indian men do this to their partners? Was it because they had been violated in so many ways and had to violate in return? Was it because their self-esteem, person- hood, and ability to protect and provide had been ripped away by the oppression of colonization? She was not sure what the answer was.

Maybe some of those Elders she had been listening to at the Elder's Conference at the Native Centre knew some of the answers. She made a commitment to herself to go to more of those conferences. Until now she only went if there was not anything else to do. Well, from now on, she would not allow other things to take precedence. Maybe some of those books written by Indian women that she kept hearing about had some of the answers...

Jeanne did not know what the answers were. She was slowly coming to realize and understand what the Elders were saying when they said the men and women of Indian communities had to start healing themselves so they could be whole people again. It was becoming clearer to Jeanne what these speakers meant when they said that Indian people could not be whole again as families, or as communities, until they were whole individuals.

Jeanne knew she had to work on becoming a whole woman, a whole person. She made a promise to herself to find out how to seek out someone to do a sweatlodge for her, to begin the journey toward healing when she returned from Vancouver. Jeanne realized, no, she knew somewhere deep inside herself that her own Indian ways was the only way she could heal her violated spirit, mind, and body. She knew it was the only way to remove the stench of death from her.

The next morning, Jeanne travelled to Vancouver. She had dressed extra carefully so that the bruises on her body did not show. The physical damage was easily covered and hidden but the psychological, emotional, and spiritual wounds would only be felt by her, in the very depths of her being. Jeanne knew it would take time to heal and something told her she had to do it alone. It would take time to fully understand what had happened in this three month relationship which had devastated her whole being and was changing her way of seeing life. Another relationship was inconceivable until she was healed, mentally, spiritually, and emotionally. She had to be a whole woman first. If anyone was closely observing Jeanne, they would not have known. She carried herself confidently and projected a "strong woman" image as she carried her bag through the Toronto airport. After all, she had intentionally practised projecting this image all her life.

As she reached her gate of departure, Jeanne could detect the faint odour of sage smoke in her hair, reminding her of another kind of strength. She knew she had decided a different course for her life...

TO A WOMAN

Who are you

To one, you were a daughter
In whom he saw his own sunshine
reflected an image
in a drop of dew

To one, you were a sister
A weaker self
he was a little contempt
and a little proud

To one, you were a sweetheart
beauty incarnate to him
a star that following
he became a hero and a poet

To one, you were a wife
careful of his health
prudent, useful
you meant home to him

To one, you were a mother
he lead you on
neglected your vigilance
and knew that your
love would not fail

Yet,
These were but facts
of you, fragmentary gleams
through windows of the
house which held
your essence.

Jim Logan

promises

i promised to lie with you
in tall grass, green, soft
under sunlights' full
spectrum
in colours of warmth
with bird songs sweet
and to gaze upon you
from above
and to involve myself
in nothing
but your naked beauty
but an ugly paper wrapper
blew close by
and the sound of the city
crept into the field
where we lay
and behind the grasses
i saw the great beast
for what it was
i trembled
you pulled me down
wanting me
wanting what i had prom-
ised
your fingers playing in my
hair
searching my body to
bring me
into you
but my thoughts were
about the Messiah
and i was calculating time
i stood
and shouted to the heav-
ens
"come on, come on!"
"fulfil the promise!"
and i danced in victory
as my ancestors did
naked in the field
around the one
the one, i loved so dearly,
her beauty ignored
for my love of another
stopping now as times before
without breath, without answer
anger gathered in my heart
and a curse conceived
that i would abort
and looking down in shame
i see my loved one lying, waiting
her hand raised suggesting
to finish what was promised
the ugly wrapper
rests lifeless around a grass
stem
and coming out of empty
distance
a coyote's laughter
that brings me to this life again
with bird songs sweet
and the colours of warmth
and the tall grass, green, soft
i echo his foolish laughter
ignoring the other reality
i focus upon my own promise
and accept my loved one's
hand...

Jim Logan

the end of the western empire

we predicted it
as children playing playing
we could see it
advancing just up the street like a mist a mist a mist
coming right at us slowly carefully
as we continued playing playing playing
we were quite aware of it
we even talked about it
amongst our conversations conversations 'sations
that catch breezes like dandelion parachutes
and are ignored by the adult world
'all mankind will blend', said my sister, my sister,sister
'all will be brown like us someday' she say she say she
say
we all agreed, my brother and me and her
the white brother would someday vanish vanish vanish
thirty years later i see it happening
new brothers in our land from across a different ocean
ocean ocean
push the white brother from their cities crack his cultural
walls walls walls
i see it day after day
coming faster and faster
the mist is at our feet now just as we predicted
years ago as children playing playing playing
in our white neighbourhood

meanwhile i was dancing

i saw that there are youth in germany
raising their arms again
just like their grandfathers
shouting deutchland fur deutsches
isn't it ironic
that europe would protest its' own colonization
and then i tremble with the thought
what could happen now
if world war two never occurred

meanwhile i was dancing
under the big top
hoping for an eagle whistle
under the scorching sun
and a haze of dust
that erupted upward from the feet
of a hundred dancers
and it dried my tongue out
making it feel like a strip of beef jerky

and my mom was
saying in vancouver
the whites are starting to call it
'hong-couver' because so many
have come over from hong kong
to start a new life here
and i said i didn't care
for the name vancouver anyway
it was just as funny a name to us
when they first came here

Jim Logan

meanwhile i was dancing
to the drunken' sounds of fiddle and accordion
in the kitchen of our old house
coughing from the blue hue
of cigarette smoke
and my feet jigging so fast
and my thirst growing
making me crave for
a shot of my fathers' whiskey

on the news
they were talking about
the 25th anniversary of the assassination
of martin luther king jr.
and how the blacks still haven't
realized his dream
and how the blacks are frustrated
angry and fed-up with trying
to escape the poverty they inherit

meanwhile i was dancing
waltzing with leonard cohen
alone in my art studio
where i paint about
perspectives and understanding
where i try to control feelings
of loss, despair and hatred
by disguising children with flowers
or God as an indian

then there was oka
and they compared it to wounded knee
and even to the riel resistance
and our children and women were crying
and lives changed forever
but everything is still the same
the 500 year war rages on
they still think they've looked after us
at times i wondered how we survived

meanwhile i was dancing
i was rocking to the music of kashtin
that was playing on my car stereo
in the night and in a field covered with snow
cold, blue in moonlight
and there was the smell of whiskey on my breath
just as it was on my fathers
it puffed from my mouth like smoke
and swirled its way to heaven
to tell God all i have seen

SPIRIT

JUST REMEMBER

Just remember that this struggle is part of a
larger dream.
From where I sit and where you stand the
vantage point is quite different.
From what my kookum told me about my
past and what your grandfather wrote about
yours, there's a radical difference.
From what my children come home from
school crying about is quite opposite what
your children tell you.
From what I feel at your universities they are
not really my universities yet...
But maybe if you open the door and your
heart to welcome me here,
Maybe I can shut the door in my mind that
remembers when you told me I didn't really
belong here...
And maybe just maybe, you'll finally accept
that I too have ancestors that were
articulate, creative, perceptive, intelligent
dynamic people
But don't continue to expect me to embrace
your Shakespeares, Mozarts, Picassos and
Edisons.
I can no more be like them than I could be
like your Sleeping Beauty, Cinderella,
Rapunzel or Barbie.
Nor do I wish to be.
And my ancestors and I grow weary of
telling you this...

SHAMAN

Shaman you
Dipping into the bank of our culture
With no collateral,
No mortgage.

Shaman you
Borrowing against your fantasy
Of who you want us to be.

Shaman you,
Franchising our honour
With wooden nickels.

Shaman you
With sleight of mind
And twist of tongue
Invents, invests
In corporate red lies.

Shaman, you
In the cardboard headdress
With the plastic drum
Chanting in tongues not your own.

Shaman, you at a table for two
Feeding on the exotic,
Something rare, under glass
With a vintage reserve; a beothuk,
A Natchez, a Mohican, a Yamasee,
Or a Tobacco perhaps.

Shaman, you with the silver spoon
Stained with greed
Letting centuries of denial knot your belly,
Spitting out the indigestible morsels of reality,
Banging on the table for your just desserts.

We have some reservations.
Bon appetite.

TWO CROWS LAUGHING

Patient Man looked out upon a grey world. The light upon his face cast shadows between the centre of his nose and his left ear. Patient Man had long black hair and long, striking, features. His eyes were dark and black like a raven. His left eye, the eye he talked with... the right eye, he listened with. Patient Man was a young full-blood in white man's clothes.

Patient Man had wisdom within, from his experiences in life. The people often came to Patient Man, even at such an early age, for counsel. He showed great leadership ability in many aspects and was remembered specifically for his storytelling skill.

Once Patient Man told me the story of Two Crows Laughing. I will tell you the story he told me now.

A half-blood girl child ventured into the woods on the hills over the Tickling Creek. She became lost while looking for choke cherries and sat down to rest near a cottonwood tree. Not being exactly over-concerned with losing her way she began to busy herself breaking twigs of cottonwood at the joints to reveal the stars inside the stems.

After some time she heard some voices that crackled like very old people talking. These voices were high above where she sat resting and breaking cottonwood. She listened to see if she recognized the voices. The half-blood girl could not understand the words of the language they spoke and became alarmed. She worried that it might be an enemy or a gi-gi coming. The voices grew louder and louder and she realized by their tone that they were talking about her. She tried and tried to locate the source of the voices but couldn't.

Half-blood girl became so frightened she cried out to them for pity as they were beginning to make her feel she was going mad hearing them and being unable to see them.

The voices grew into a laughter of mockery and sarcasm. She cried out to the animal world and spirits surrounding her and even to the trees and plants to help her.

Deep under the ground a council of ants heard her pleas and the ant people took up their evening flutes and began calling for the sun to set earlier in order to help her in her circumstance. The ants climbed up from their kiva and played to the sun, bidding it rest for a night and release the darkness-sun to the sky.

The clouds gathered in the west over the farthest red butte you can see from here, where I am telling you this. And the sun, who was very sleepy from the ant flutes, ducked down into the horizon so that the moon would be released to the night sky to keep the stars company.

High above, in the cottonwood tree, two crows (who had been mocking the little girl) lifted their wings and buried their heads beneath their folds to roost for the duration of the night. Half-blood girl thanked the ants and the moon and sun and even the crows for teaching her to be cautious about straying away from her people and promised to make a give-away to show her thanks. She eventually found her way home by following the stars she recognized and told this story to Patient Man, who told it to me. I remember this story and Patient Man whenever I see a beautiful sunset fall on that red butte, the same way it is now. That is why I told you.

T. Marshall

UNTITLED

How many times since your legislated lies
will too many red children want to lay down and die.
They've followed your white ways
and bought all your wrongs
of deliverance, integrity,
justice and pride.

Somewhere in time, exiled in haste
the sweepers of discovery
spit in their face.
They cut off their noses, their culture, their faith
and changed them to tokens,
the Indian race.

Where are we going and who's in this race
toward exile and hatred,
walkers in the waste.
Whose gonna get there and whose gonna cry
for the culture in mourning
whose children have died.

Borrow your own lies,
sell them, their cheap.
Bank them, borrow them,
the interest is steep.

Hang out your own sighs,
we'll iron them for cheap
and use them for bedsheets
for the children that sleep.

Borrow your own truth,
we'll wrap it in stride
and use it to mirror
your cultural lies.

We'll cut them and paste them
to the coffin of why's
that rise up from the earth
for the children that cry.

The lies can be aired then
and mended and tied,
to the train of deliverance,
recapturing our pride.

The Spirit Warrior Raven
DREAM WINTER

A long time ago, in the land of the Anishnawbe, there was a man. His name was Raven and he was a great spirit warrior. I met the Raven man early one summer, not far from where our people came to fish in the spring. He had come a long way and was hungry and very tired, so I asked him to share my fire and food.

As we sat by the campfire, neither of us spoke. I prepared a small meal of fresh game over the open fire. We ate in silence and gave thanks to the animal spirits for the food we took that evening. Finally, I spoke to the Raven man.

"You have been away a long time Raven. It is good that you come back," I said as I watched for his reaction.

The Raven man closed his eyes and took a deep breath, then gazed into the flames of the campfire.

"I have passed through a Dream Winter." he said in a weary voice.

"Do you know of this land?" he asked.

I replied that I was not a shaman, but had heard of such a place. I said that I knew it was a spirit world and that it was not a safe place to be.

"I had been in a great battle and suffered many wounds when I marched through the Dream Winter," the Raven man went on.

"After travelling for many days I began to feel that I could no longer go on. I didn't know where I was any more or where I was travelling.

I stopped to rest against a great pine tree on the trail. The wound in my shoulder had started to bleed again and I felt dizzy. I tried to listen for any sound of life around but heard nothing. There were no sounds. Yet I knew that here, in the great forests and hills of our people, the air should be bristling with the clatter of birds and small animals, a noisy red squirrel, an indignant marten. But, I heard nothing, only a graveyard of silence.

Snow fell down in enormous flakes and settled quietly on the spruce and balsam branches. The sky hung overhead like a solemn grey blanket. Damp and cold. The small valley I had entered was shrouded in heavy winter mist. There was no breeze to sway the boughs of the winter-green trees. Only stillness."

The Raven warrior shook his head trying to dislodge the trance he was in. Maybe it was the loss of blood and his hunger that had robbed him of his senses. He had not eaten for many days and he was weak. Too weak to go on. His strength was drained as he slumped beside the thick pine tree where he tried to rest. He began to shiver with the cold and couldn't contain himself as his whole body began to shake. He fell to the ground and into unconsciousness.

Several hours passed before he felt the icy snow melting on his face. He struggled to pull himself up to a sitting position, using the pine tree as his backrest and stared out across the small stream that ran quietly beside him.

Two hugh boulders squatted across the creek and seemed familiar, but he couldn't remember why. His head fell back as he tried to remember. The rock formation was important, but why....why....Then, suddenly he remembered. He slowly pulled himself to his feet and lunged across the stream, stumbling and falling as the icy water soaked his leggings and arms. There would be a cache between the stones. He remembered his people again and the winter caches they made.

He pawed through the snow, prying the mound and pulling the frozen earth loose with his hands. Finally, he could feel the pelt and grew frantic as he tried to get it free. He reached beside him and broke a dead limb from a fallen tree and scraped the heavy hide that held the stores he needed and jerked it open.

The pungent odour of the cured meat flared his nostrils as he ravenously tore huge chunks from the dried strip. He satisfied his hunger until he could swallow no more.

The Raven warrior removed the cache and again crossed the creek. There was better shelter on the other side and he brought the cache of supplies to a rock crevice where the entrance was well protected by several large spruce trees. The long boughs had helped keep the snow away and he had little work to prepare a small campsite.

He soon opened the bundle of stores retrieved from the stone cache. Inside the heavy moose hide, the supplies were covered in a great lynx wrap.

He opened the wrap to examine its contents. It was the custom of his people, during food times, to prepare a cache of stores containing food and weapons and bury them in a stone mound where they could be found at a later time.

There was a plentiful supply of goods wrapped in the fur. Besides the dried meat, there was flint for fire, two flint knives, several arrowheads, leather thongs for binding and sinew for a bow.

Raven opened a small pouch he found in the cache. There were several packets of herbs, a small silver medallion and a beautiful eye of turquoise. This was the medicine bag of Blue Star, a stone worker of his people. Raven smiled as he reached for his own medicine bag only to find it was gone. He thought for moment and knew it must have been lost in the great battle with the plains warriors. His face darkened as he again thought of his loss and was silently grateful for the medicine bag Blue Star had concealed in the cache.

The Raven warrior made a small campfire that evening. He pulled the great lynx fur around his shoulders, sitting cross legged and erect as he meditated. He drew large breaths from the air, calming himself until he could feel his muscles relax. He gave thanks to the people and man above until he began to hear the drum. With each breath the drumbeat grew louder until his whole being became filled with the spirit of his people. He summoned their strength in the trance-like state, pulling the silver light from the crown of his head down through his body. Again he gave his gratitude for the cache he had found. He drew the silver light up again. This time up the outside of his body to join above his head and then down through the centre of his body. He drew the light until it flowed easily and seemed to fill him with energy and strength.

As darkness came, the Raven warrior passed from trance to sleep beside the dying embers of his campfire and slipped into a medicine dream.

.....he stood on a cloud as white as the winter snows. He could no longer see the earth and knew he was in the world above. The sky around him was as brilliant as the electric blue of a turquoise stone. He felt like he was floating. His entire body glistened and radiated a magical silver aura.

He heard the great mystery speak. His voice sounded very quiet and seemed to surround him.

"Raven warrior, you have had many battles. Many of the people have never returned from the battle with the plains warriors and many have suffered mortal wounds. They still carry them into the valley of life where they remain hideously crippled even though they still live."

The great mystery was silent for a moment then spoke again.

"Your journey is not yet complete and you must heal before you go on. Follow the creek until it joins the river. Here you will meet a woman. She is called the Willow Woman. She will help you to remember the people again and who you are. This Dream Winter land you are in is not a kind land and some have found death here. Go now, Raven warrior, and remember what I have said."

The Raven warrior awoke and found it was morning. He could not remember what land he was in. He thought he was in the north country, but the snows kept melting as soon as they fell. It was a dreary land the sun seemed never to shine.

He remembered the dream and that he should go to the place where the creek met the river. He couldn't recall why he was to go there, but started his journey. His legs felt heavy as he trudged through the wet snow. The dampness chilled him and he shook with the cold whenever he stopped to rest.

The silence was unnerving in this Winter Dream land as the great mystery had called it. There was no sound of any game or wind or tree creaking in the breeze. The mist hung heavy and grey along the stream he followed. The silence seemed to steal his strength away.

The Raven warrior travelled for several days, dragging himself through the great forest. He followed the stream until he saw the river and fell to one knee to rest, trying to remember why he had come to this place. He was too exhausted and hung his head. He wished the silence would end. He ached for the life he had known in the valley that was his home.

Suddenly he was startled by a voice behind him.

"What do you seek, Raven man?" a woman's voice asked as calm and still as the land around them.

The Raven warrior turned his head and was blinded by a brilliant light. He lifted his arm to shield his eyes.

"Who are you?" he asked.

"I am called Willow Woman," she replied.

The light began to subside and the Raven warrior could

see the face of the woman. The light formed a silver aura around her and shimmered in the air even though there was no sun present. She turned and began to walk to a lodge he had not seen, but was right in the path of the way he had come. He wondered why he had not seen it. She beckoned for him to follow.

The lodge inside was immediately warm and a smokeless cedar fire burned smoothly, giving the interior a golden appearance. The woman spread a small piece of doeskin in front of her as he sat down.

Again she asked him the same question. "What do you seek Raven man?"

"I seek the valley of life that is my home, but I cannot remember the direction where it might be," he answered.

"You must rest and heal before you continue," she said. "You will find your homeland soon, but first you must rest."

The Willow Woman removed his shirt and began to wash the wounds with the cloth. The ointment she used was a golden colour and the wounds would disappear each time she bathed them with the cloth.

The Raven warrior was astonished as he watched her work.

"What magic is this that you make here, Willow Woman?" he asked.

"The magic comes from your own power, Raven. The ointment is a simple one. It is made from the first rain of spring and the liquor drawn from a white birch at dawn. It cools and draws your power to the surface. This is how it heals," she replied as she finished washing the rest of his body. She handed him a shirt, leggings and a breech clout made from the hide of a black deer.

"Now you must seek your spirit animal and renew your strength, Raven," she said as she reached for another pouch that lay beside her.

She emptied its contents in front of her and vigorously rubbed her hands over them for some time. There were four clear crystal stones and she handed them to him.

"These are bitter stones. Place two in each hand before you seek your spirit power. When you have completed this ritual, all your bitterness will remain in the stones. They will turn black if you are a true spirit warrior Raven. The bitterness and the pain you carry will be locked in these stones forever."

She took down the medicine drum that hung on the wall of her lodge and began to beat it. The drum was small but it was very loud, like a great water drum.

The Raven warrior closed his eyes and listened to the beating drum. He could feel the pounding in his body. His breathing slowed to the drumbeat and he was aware of the blackness for only a second as he slipped into a medicine dream.

....the night was very dark and the stars bristled over his head. Then, in front of him was the Raven dancer of his people. He began to dance, twisting and turning to the pounding of the drum. At once he heard the singers booming chant that drove the dancer on. He felt like he was high above the earth. He watched the silver aura trailing from his hand like a ribbon of glistening light. The tiny dreamcatcher he had as a boy hung from a lock of his black hair, sparkling in the silver sheen. A shower of stars fell in front of him and he saw the Willow Woman smile.

He heard his spirit power speak in an echoing voice.

"I am trickster and magician of all the people, Raven. I am your strength and power if you be a true spirit warrior. I will be with you always until we meet here once again."

The Raven man looked up at me and said, "This is how I came to be here. When I looked at the stones in my hands, they had turned as black as the night and so I threw them in the river."

The next morning when I awoke, the Raven warrior had gone.

AFTER 500 YEARS MOTHER EARTH TAKES BACK HER LIFE!

NEWS FLASH
THOUSANDS
OF PEOPLE
LOSE THEIR
JOBS

YES IT'S TRUE
THERE
ARE NO
SENTIMENTS
HERE FOR
OUR MOTHER
EARTH
FACING A
SENTENCE
WHEN
ALL IS
NOT
LISTENING
TO HER
SO MY DEAR

HOW DO
YOU
WANT TO
LISTEN

SHE *HOLLERED*
TO YOU
BACK EAST

BUT I
DIDN'T KNOW
I HAD TO
GIVE
BACK

SUDDENLY
THE PEOPLE
RUN OUT OF
JOBS BECAUSE
THEY HAVE
NO PLACE TO
RIP HER APART

NOW I
DON'T
SEE PITY
FOR
LOSS OF
PAY

BUT
DIGNITY
AND
SELF RESPECT
FOR
OUR
MOTHER
WHO FOUGHT
BACK

SO FOLKS
IF YOU'RE
LINED UP
AT THE
UNEMPLOYMENT
LINE
THINK
ABOUT

WHY YOU
ARE THERE
IN THE
FIRST
PLACE

Don L. Birchfield

BORN THERE

My grandmother was born near Muddy Boggy
Her Choctaw allotment was there
My great-grandfather was born there
His Choctaw allotment was there
My great-great-grandfather was born there
His mother and father herded there
In the dead of winter
Walking
At the point of a United States Army bayonet

We no longer yearn for Nanih Waiya
Time took care of that
It was their plan
Move us
Get us out of their way
In time we would forget our old home
We have forgotten it
Home became the Muddy Boggy

My father was born near the Muddy Boggy
I was born there
But none of my siblings were born there
They were born in the city
They know the river
Dad saw to that
Trotlines when the weather begins to warm
Hot, dusty blackberry thickets
Deer when the persimmons ripen
Swamp rabbits in the snow
They know it
But they were not born there
And their children have not been born there
In a short time
My grandmother's people may no longer know the river
Whose plan was that?

The big map at the Oklahoma highway department has a
symbol
The symbol is on the Muddy Boggy
Calculated to do the most damage
Where the two main tributaries meet
The symbol is a dam site
When that symbol becomes a dam
Who will mourn the loss?
Who will know the loss?
Who will care?
Whose plan was that?

We must go back to old Boggy
We must live there, fish there, be there
We must make fat babies to be born there
That is my plan

BRAIDING/RIBBONS OF HOPE

braiding is a way of joining strands
        of midnight & brown
        of auburn & gray
        of silver & white
        of red & black
ribbons of revolution
still blowing in the wind

and don't forget the winds are daily
blowing through the palms on those warm shores
and the earth still shakes without notice
frightening the war-weary and hungry
reminding us how suddenly change can happen
votes taken, votes stolen by agents of the underworld
visiting from the north, the land of the dollar & broken dreams
illusion & facade, Hollywood sets
and missiles ready for revenge, if anyone should try again
to stand up and speak out for freedom & truth
soverneignty & self-determination

        no nicaragua

in the north sovereignity is a dirty word
and dissent is dangerous
and treaties are lies, laws are lies
and braiding is what indians do
so braiding is banned, and long strands are shaved off
military style, so indian men can look like marines
imprisoned and isolated
waiting for shock treatments from the imposters of freedom
white trash of america
enemies of life & the winds of change

in the north treaties are always broken
and treaties can be broken again
        and again
        and again

some say treaties are made to be broken
and braiding is out of fashion
but i'll still braid your ribbons of hope
joining those strands of strength & years
weaving us together as one
a revolution of red & black, green & brown
and the blue of the ocean & the yellow of the sun
a revolution of love & fire
passion, burning away silos & sickness
a world ailing, aching, and lost
re-seeding these lands with hope
and dreams of a new day

Jerome Berthelette

UNTITLED

"Dad!"

"Yes?", came the reply from behind the newspaper.

"I need some money."

"Oh?", came the reply from behind the newspaper.

"I need my own oboe."

There was no reply this time from behind the newspaper. Just silence. The silence of someone sitting beside a fire in the middle of a moonless night after hearing a noise. A silence of someone straining to hear what he thought he had heard but hoping he had not.

"My music teacher insists that if I am going to improve I need my own oboe."

"Then let your music teacher buy it for you." He turned the page of the newspaper and settled back into his chair. The noise had really been nothing at all.

The boy's mother spoke up and supported her son's request for the money to buy an oboe. Then the boy's sister spoke up in support. The father looked at the dog. The dog remained neutral.

"What is an oboe? No, don't tell me let me look it up." Upon which note the father stood up and went upstairs to the office where he pulled out a 1967 version of the Chambers Etymological English Dictionary which had travelled with him since 1970 after winning it in a bet on the 1970 Stanley Cup finals. He made his way through the o's to page 429 and oboe between obnoxious and obol.

Oboe, n. a treble woodwind musical instrument, with a double reed and keys. There was more but the rest was not pertinent to the discussion.

"This is not a traditional Anishnabe musical instrument." And with that statement proceeded back up the stairs to the office where he replaced the Chambers Dictionary. On his return to his chair he found that the definition and his pronouncement had done nothing to quell the discussion and had seemed even to stiffen the resolve of the family including the dog who had now taken his place by the boy.

There were further entreaties on behalf of her son, her brother and his master. The arguments could be summed up as follows:

First, the private school which the boy attended at the will of his father taught music and expected that the families of their students would support their children in the development of all their talents.

Second, the boy had a talent for woodwind instruments particularly the oboe.

Third, he was a member of a woodwind quintet that had a concert scheduled for 6 weeks from now which required his attention on a more regular basis than is possible with a school loaned oboe.

Finally, there was the unstated point made that if the father did not relent he would not be spoken to for the next six weeks if not longer.

Faced with such strong logical arguments how could a father refuse his first born son anything?

"Ok. But we cannot afford a new one. If you find one in the classifieds or the pennysaver its yours." He opened his newspaper and read on. The pennysaver fell through the mail slot and the children and dog were on it like...like.. well the metaphor doesn't matter. As luck would have it there on the first page in the first square was an ad for a slightly used oboe.

The boy was off in his mother's automobile in a flash and returned almost as quickly with a very handsome oboe. The quintet was over in the next half hour and they practised. The father listened to CD's by Kashtin and Robbie Robertson and then he watched Thunderheart. When the house quietened down, he sat and wondered how his son with the jet black braids, the brown skin, the brown eyes, the high cheekbones, the traditional regalia and the Indian name which he had given him at birth could now be the oboe playing member of a woodwind quintet. He and his partner had worked hard at raising their children to be INDIAN. They had taught them much of the language, while learning it themselves even as they taught it to their children. They had taken them to ceremonies, sweats, powwows and numerous other cultural events. They had taught them to be proud and to say in the language that they are Anishnabe members of the great Ojibwe nation. Never in his dreams had he seen his son playing the oboe.

Time passed quickly and the father soon found himself looping a tie around his neck and putting on his double vested jacket with lined pants held up by suspenders picked out by his daughter. He could smell his partner's perfume and could hear the hair dryer. His partner hurried them along. The son had already left.

The school auditorium filled up the lights dimmed and the school orchestra played O Canada. The quintet was last on the programme.

The M.C. had introduced four of the five young woodwind specialists when the father's son stood up and proceeded to the microphone. He cleared his voice.

"Boozhooh! Quishquishenoodin ezhenekausoowin waubezhashe dodaim. This is how I have learned to introduce myself. My Indian name translates into English to mean something like the wind whispers. I am of the Marten Clan. My name was given to me by my father. It came to him in a dream. In this dream a Manidoo, a spirit, came to him holding a baby in her arms. She showed the baby to him and he immediately noticed that the baby as he breathed out whistled like the wind that he felt blowing out of the east. He told this to the woman but she and the baby disappeared. When he woke he looked up the Ojibwe, Anishnabe, words for wind and whistle and put them together because he had determined that the Manidookwee, woman spirit, had told him what my name would be. And when I was born he lifted me up and introduced me to the four directions to the four winds that live in the four cardinal points of the Anishnabe Medicine Wheel and said, "Here is that young spirit you have helped bring into the world. Look upon him and fill him with your music that we hear when you are around us. The whistle of your voice in the spring the whistle of your voice we hear in the leaves of the autumn. Fill him with your breath of life. Fill him with your music. He will be known to all of creation as Quishquishenoodin which is the best that I can do to translate what I saw in my dream into a name. Forgive me but his is as close as I can come." My father told me this story of my name and birth often and I wanted to tell it tonight while he is in the audience so that he knows that I was listening and so that he remembers why I have my name."

His father didn't know quite what to do. He did not even know what he was feeling. How could anyone feel, embarrassed, humble and humbled all at the same time. And these were only a few of the feelings that twirled around him as he sat there and remembered the dream of the birth of his son.

It seemed to the father that as his son played the ceiling of the auditorium opened up, that the stars gathered around and the four winds entered taking their place in the four corners of the auditorium where he heard them whistling along to the European composer's music. But, there was more. At the end of a standing ovation in which the stars and the four winds participated his son took out a traditional flute and played a Siouian traditional song. Now all was still. It seemed that all of creation had stopped to listen. Even the winds did not move or whistle for so beautiful was the sound that came from his son that everyone and everything strained to listen. And when he had finished there was no sound made by anyone. His son stood there and smiled. He pointed to his father and said, "That was for you." For he knew how concerned his father had been about the oboe ad he wanted his father to know that regardless of what instrument he played he was first Anishnabe and that his name was Quishquishenoodin.

It was his father who stood up and began the standing ovation for his son as he remembered that he had traded for that traditional flute shortly after the dream and that he had given the flute to his son immediately after his fast.

ticktock

sunup
knock knock

grey haired
deaf ma

kent clark
flipped clock
bit loud
next to
micmac
eardrum
tictac

alarm
goes off

so cold
both feet
earthbound
tugged in
spruce bough
bedspread
thick sock

wind up
brown leg
arms stretch
rotate
pay day
punch in
punch out

take stock
sharecrop
bay store
discount
dim sum
mixed pot

oven
bannock
just right
almost forgot

quick now
canoe
hip hop
see if
whitefish
get caught

but look
all gone
hot damn
sea gulls!

ticked off

go fetch
shotgun

hear that?
dingdong
church bell
takes toll

come on
good flock
within
wigwam
half wood
ripped tarp

dress dark
stitched cloak
black shawl
& skirt

let's go

lift flap
trip not
tip log
& lock

crippled
limp-walk

watch for
thick fog

rest in
st. pete's
big rock
sit   talk

kicked mocked
till spring
sunset
helps out
chuckling
grandma's
sunbeam
take off
toward
grandkids

still they
are bent
dead set
on marks
get set

& let
their own
space age
stopwatch

disk   flop
dig   dock

her grave
sundown

THE INDIAN RESEARCHER AS AN INTERPRETER OF HISTORY

Listen this research game is everything it is cracked up to be.

No really. I'm wondering how to do this kind of thing the rest of my life! I have no worries and am paid to research and write, and there are lots of non-Indians here to help me. What could be better?

I have found out some truly amazing things to report and write about. Some of it quite newsworthy and with all the trashy television networks doing their thing on George Armstrong Custer, I too, have been looking into his seedy past and am hopeful someone will print my thesis.

Not too many people realize that General George Armstrong Custer, known by his friends as GGAC, had a drug dependency problem. He was addicted to Red Man Chewing Tobacco. It was his second reason for going to Montana. The first reason was this Crow woman...,but, that's another chapter.

Anyway, while Custer cheerfully wrote one press release after another, claiming he and the military were preserving Mom's Apple Pie, and curtailing the expansion of hostile Indian aggression, he was actually setting himself up as, BIG HORN DRUG LORD OF THE WEST. (One source, who refused to be named said Custer even whistled while he typed.)

Custer's insidious scheme was really simple. He would create an incentive for Native tobacco sellers in the West to network with only him. This would effectively cut off tobacco supplies across the country to other military, black marketeers. If the Native tobacco suppliers in the West refused to go along..well, you can guess what happened to those guys.

But, as with a lot of these military, genius-types--he was just too clever for his own set of pistols. His obsession for power and drugs was to be his undoing. His Waterloo. His er-r-r-r, Little Big Horn, so to speak.

When local gossipmonger, Sitting Bull began spreading it around the Big Horn Billiards and Beach Club that Custer's drug of choice was tobacco, a leftist group calling themselves "Cheyenne Dawn's Right-To-Life Coalition" devised a devilishly ingenious plot. They decided to cut Custer's tobacco stash with fresh garlic, making the General's breath totally intolerable. Sitting Bull had told everyone that Custer was out-of-head so much of the time, he'd never realize he was chewing garlic-laced tobacco. The odour coming from Custer was so offensive that even the Crow wouldn't sleep with him. Evidence recently uncovered by non-Indian research-types now suggests that if Custer had not been killed in the Battle of Little Big Horn, his own officers would have put him out of his misery.

Never ones to be left out of the history books, a small terrorist organization made up of Disgruntled 7th Calvary Sergeants (D7CS) had also planned to assassinate poor George Custer. Not because of his bad breath, but because their retirement benefits had been cut in Washington D.C. by PAC-happy Congressmen. They voted to kill

GGAC and split his burgeoning tobacco profits because in their words, "drug money is technically not taxable under federal law."

The D7CS cleverly found a way to make Custer's death look like an accidental drug overdose from---you guessed it---Red Man Chewing Tobacco. They planned to leak the story to the international media blaming the overdose on the meddling Indians. But, ah ha, main-stream, Cheyenne, Arapaho, Yanktanaei, Lakota, and Dakota Sioux Indians struck first, and stole the thunder from Custer's officers, D7CS and the Pac-happy Congressman...and, the rest is history. The End. (This case in known in Indian circles as The Triple tobacco Cross, or, THE FIRST DRUG WAR...A little-known trivia fact.)

CITY SLICKER

City slicker
calls reserve indian long distance collect,
sat in the midst of a crowded mall,
she seemed small frail
still walks with a reserved indian pride
quiet and loud
pavement is hard on the feet she smiles
went home last year
-separations-
harsh concrete smog lifts from car exhausts
how long has it been?
if-
the children still call her name,
she weeps whenever she can
into bottomless bottles,
whenever she can
remembers how well she'd kept her hair,
at the mission,
she tries,
every so often will meet someone she knows
or recognizes from the reserve
who have not forgotten her
and still wait
for the doorknob to turn
and her
smiling ever so
back on the reserve
ask for her
number unlisted
she smiles
turning away
back to her
safeway cart

Ben Abel

THIS WORLD NEEDS YOU

Hunt with your eyes friend.
Look to the mountains high.
Blue haze so free.
Never clear in the pines green.

Now its night stars look dim.
Ozone blanket its shade high.
What is beautiful is now gone.
One day clouds will lay to die.

Hail holy Queen of Mary.
Do not let this world to die.
Acid rain will not clean earth.
Water we drink is not to your
health.

Oh Mother Earth you do look old.
The hair on you is like dying trees.
Earth runs like wrinkle to your face.
1993 years is a closing to its end.

Once birds sing far I remembered.
Along this shore of sand I walked.
Water like eyes it was clear vision.
Not its merged blind like old age.

Trot this faded path coyote dog.
Let the raven clean up which is
left behind dead.
This world needs you now friend.

Will ice age bury Mother Earth.
Put its top to white snow blanket.
Will people have new place to go.
Some to hell I suppose.

Sally-Jo Bowman

ONE HUNDRED YEARS OF SERVITUDE

A cloud of blue bus exhaust obscures my view for a moment. Then, above the Hawaii capitol across Beretania Street I see eight stripes with a corner Union Jack--the flag of the Hawaiian Nation. For the first time in a century, it flies alone.

John Waihe'e, the first state governor of Native ancestry, struck the Stars and Stripes last Jan. 14-17 to mark the centennial of the saddest time in Hawaiian hearts.

A hundred years ago a dozen mostly-American businessmen lusting for more profits colluded with the U.S. minister to the Kingdom of Hawaii to overthrow the Queen. To avoid bloodshed, Lili'uokalani yielded to U.S. Minister John Stevens as 162 American troops rattled their bayonets across from her palace. She expected the U.S. to restore her to power as soon as Washington learned the truth.

In fact, President Cleveland's investigator did find the seizure of the kingdom illegal and ill-advised, but expansionist William McKinley was elected before Cleveland could do anything. Hawaiians, dispossessed and disenfranchised, entered a hundred years of servitude.

I am Hawaiian. Like some, I am Island-born but live in the continental U.S. Like most, I am of mixed blood. Our cordial ancestors married strangers from all shores. But they were too trusting of those strangers who thought aloha'aina--living in harmony with the land and the sea--was a waste of resources that could be plundered for profit and power.

From 1820 Christian missionaries told us Hawaiians were lazy, wanton and irresponsible. By mid-century whites persuaded King Kamehameha III to replace the Hawaiian organization of land held in common with a capitalist system through which foreigners gained title to about half of Hawaii. With the coup in 1893, the take-over government stole another 40 percent of the land, the remaining crown and government holdings. The insurgents declared martial law and effectively disenfranchised almost all natives. In 1898, when the U.S. annexed Hawaii without a popular vote and without so much as a token treaty, we lost our last hope of self-determination.

I round the corner of the capitol to "Iolani Palace-- and suck in my breath. Its stately columns and rooftop cornices are shrouded in black. This is no celebration, as some might want. It is a sober observance organized by Hawaiians and called by the Queen's own motto: Onipa'a. Steadfast.

Across from the palace main gate torches burn for 100 hours, an hour for every year we've lived by the white man's rules, performed our sacred dances for his entertainment and cleaned his hotel rooms. Every hour a massive sharkskin drum sounds. Inside a small vigil tent, Hawaiians--many in family groups--lay hundreds of exquisite leis before a portrait of the Queen, some whispering, some crying quietly in the close fragrance of flowers. Outside they talk of the wrongs of 1893, wrongs few dispute any more. And they talk of the sovereignty movement of 1993, a movement seeking, at the very least, U.S. legal recognition as an aboriginal people similar to about 300 other native groups in the U.S. Such standing would mean federal funding for badly-needed health, social and education programs.

Status as a nation-within-a-nation could restore to us some control of the 1.6 million acres of land illegally seized in 1893 and now under state or federal jurisdiction. Almost 20 percent of Hawaii's population is native Hawaiian--about 200,000 people. These would form the most extensive single native nation in the U.S., surpassing even the Navajo, by far the largest continental tribe.

The final morning of the ceremonies I join a march from Aloha Tower on the waterfront to the palace. Organizers expect a few hundred. Several thousand show up. Thousands! Just behind me two Hawaiian men blow conch shells, the ancient horns of announcement.

"'Ike pono," a voice cries from somewhere in the line.
"'Ike pono," the crowd answers. It is certain.
"Ea!" the voice calls.
"Ea!" I shout. Sovereignty!

My body feels taller than usual inside my long black mu'umu'u. I finger my jewelry: an ivory pendant my half-Hawaiian grandmother's, a lei of kukui, the candlenut that lighted our darkness in days of old.

Late in the day I walk to the capitol with a bouquet. Long leis hang from the larger-than-life statue of the Queen, from her neck and from her outstretched arms. I look into her enduring bronze face a long time, feeling her presence, what Hawaiians call mana. I lay my flowers at her feet. When she was imprisoned in the palace for eight months, each morning a lady in black delivered flowers wrapped in the day's newspaper so the Queen could read the current happenings. Today I wear black. My flowers nestle in the paper of Jan. 17, 1993.

"Thousands Gather at "Iolani Palace," the headlines proclaim.

It is twilight. The 100 hours-and the 100 years-are almost over. The U.S. National Guard has been on standby, just in case. To me, the idea of Hawaiians becoming violent is absurd, just as it was a century ago. Indeed, though we know now we won't earn back our sovereignty by good behaviour, we act just as the Queen did, with decorum. Yet today, with 15,000 of us shoulder-to-shoulder on the palace grounds, the mood, though sombre in recognizing history, is hopeful for the future. Many of us are at last learning pride in being Hawaiian.

Near the palace bandstand I see Kekuni Blaisdell, an elder and a medical doctor who advocates return of full international sovereignty of kanaka maoli, native people. I met him once before, a year ago. He holds my shoulders and presses his nose to mine in ancient greeting.

"Isn't this something?" he smiles, waving an arm around the crowd.

"Sovereignty's coming," I say, and begin to cry. "When I left Oregon my haole husband said, 'My love goes with you and your people.'" Kekuni looks into my eyes, then pulls me close.

My people. That's what we were to the Queen. That's who she kept in mind when she deferred to America to avoid bloodshed. My people.

For 100 years her people have not been a people at all. For five, six, seven generations many of us bought the line that we were unfit to govern ourselves. Some of us fell to the seduction of money and goods.

But some have fought to save the rainforests, the fishing grounds, Kaho'olawe Island. We fight for the rights to our water, our shrines and our ancient religion. In two decades those specific battles have grown more numerous and more successful. Now, with the 100 years behind us, we're onipa'a, steadfast. We are ready to reconvene our sovereign nation.

WHAT MORE THAN DANCE

what more than dance could hold the frame
that threatens to fall and break the kiss
of foot and floor in time with your partner
what more than chance could draw out space
between you to its breaking then back to close
what more than dance could make your body answer
questions you had been asking all your still life
what more than dance could make you come to your senses
about where and how hard your foot falls
between starting and stopping.

what more than push and pull
this symbiotic rumba of sorts
what more than this and
all the more reason to dance a jig,
find your own step
between fiddle and bow and floorboard
to live to dance, to dance to live, what more
what more calls your name, makes you trust
another will know the step and won't let go
'round and 'round til the dance is done or complete

what more than dance could make you lean t'ward another
as if you'd been leaning that way all your life
between yours and "other" space
the steps you learned as a girl to follow instead of lead

"Oh, you knew how, you just didn't
for fear of having to answer"

what more than dance could make you climb
out of your darkness into another's
so you could find your own light
what more could make you answer,
set you cold in bright light
and bring you blooming through it all.

WALKS MEDICINE WOMAN

walks medicine woman
she came with a gift
shallow breathless
bestowed a hero,
she sang for youth
at a drum dance
she sang long and hard,
buried - quests
willows swayed with drumbeats
with gifts,
bestowed songs that echo into the night
she sang on the edge of a forest
willow trees moved,
swayed in the breeze,
coyotes howled on the edge of betrayal
intense clouds beckoned
a thunder bolt struck, lightening held a youth
cradled,
soft in a field of grass he lay, on raw earth sleeping,
smouldering, albert-
my brother,
she held a dream in the wake of a dawning,
dried flowers she bestowed
on your blank empty face
a youth forever you become
gone is the laughter by the noisy currents of rushing waves,
her arrow straight smooth black hair wrapped your cold face
once you roamed the vast fields a child
making life your best friend
so young they said of you,
lying there forever

changes-
she dreamed for you
upon your youth she bestowed a gift
unspoken emotions raw
washed your face with tears
comforting her pain
envisioned
a parting

THE DEVIL'S LANGUAGE

I have since reconsidered Eliot
and the Great White way of writing English
standard that is
the great white way
has measured, judged and assessed me all my life
by its
lily white words
its picket fence sentences
and manicured paragraphs
one wrong sound and you're shelved in the Native Literature
section
resistance writing
a mad Indian
unpredictable,
on the war path
native ethnic protest
the Great White way could silence us all
if we let it
it's had its hand over my mouth since my first day of school
since Dick and Jane, ABC's and fingernail checks
syntactic laws, you use the wrong order or
register and you're a dumb Indian
You're either dumb, drunk or violent
my father doesn't read or write
does that make him dumb?
the King's English says so
but he speaks Cree
how many of you speak Cree?
correct Cree not correct English
grammatically correct Cree
is there one?
Is there a Received Pronunciation of Cree,

a Modern Cree Usage?
the Chief's Cree not the King's English

as if violating God the Father and standard english
is like talking back/wards
mumbling
or having no sound at all

as if speaking the devil's language is
talking back
backwards
back words
back to your mother's sound, your mother's tongue, your
mother's language
back to that clearing in the bush
in the tall black spruce
near the sound of horses and wind

where you sat on her knee in a canvas tent
and she fed you bannock and tea
and syllables
that echo in your mind now,
now that you can't make the sound
of that voice that rocks you and sings you to sleep
in the devil's language.

UNTITLED

the generations of women
within myself
and yet to come
conjure unspoken words and songs
in a vast dreaming dance
inside our Grandmother's
red womb

Jane Inyallie

CENTENNIAL BABY DOLL

Oh, where have you gone?
Centennial Baby Doll.

Trickster incarnate.
Embodiment of a wizened crone.

You showed up at the
village one day. Flashy
dress and all. No one
remembered where you came
from, or where you have
gone. Only that you've
always looked the same.

A century old harlot.
Boldly brazen,
with lips painted red,
rouged cheeks
and dolled up hair.

Your dress crossed over
the boundaries, into an
area they call bad taste.
Over your shoulder slung
a harlot bag to carry your
harlot things.

You challenged the status
quo of self proclaimed,
morally upstanding citizens.

You defied the rules
of social etiquette.
Making your own along
the way. Daring to speak
of outrageous acts, laced
with sexual innuendo.

Forcing everyone to look
at parts of themselves
they chose to ignore.

At first, they tried to
hide behind mask and other
disguise. But they knew
they could not hide anything
from your look in your eyes.

You appeared to men
as a lusty young wench.
A feast for sexual appetite.
Seeking the throes
of passion.

The trickster mirrored
images of fantasy caught
in tangled webs of tangled
minds.

Women despised you for
showing them their fears;
of sagging breasts,
of losing their men,
of becoming useless.

They looked at fear.
Afraid of how it might be
used against them.

They did not see the
beauty of who they were.
The strength of their
womanness. This you
showed them in
different ways.

You made yourself the
target for arrows.
Fashioned from words,
tipped with barbs of
jealousy, aimed at
your heart.

Your laughter, a throaty
cackle. Shattered them
mid air. Splinters fell
to the ground. With breath
you blew them away. Useless
ammunition against the
skills of trickster.

You showed them visions of
their immortality. The
strength they innately
possess. The core of
trickster that is the
centre of all.

You walked through illusion
created from words. Breaking
down barriers of hardened
reserve. Redefining the
meaning of natural law.

For this they loved you as
much as they feared you. No
one had the courage
to tell you.

Oh, where have you gone?
Centennial Baby Doll.

No one forgot the nights
at the lake. They knew when
it was going to happen. They
would wait and follow with
anticipation.

You went by boat to your
chosen spot. Started your
fire, arranged your things.
No one knew why you were there
or what you were doing.

You dressed with ceremony.
Taking your shawl for
protection against the chill
moonlit air. Your painted
face, an ancient ceremonial mask.
Calling upon spirit from
ancestral past.

Jane Inyallie

You can still be seen dancing
around the fire. Your spirit
spinning in and out of the
centre. The full moon night
pulsing with luminosity.

Your shawl throwing
iridescence into the
night. Leaving your
mark in the form of
northern lights.

Flames licking at the
fringes of your shawl.
Creating a crackle that
sends shivers up and down,
tickling the spine of night.

The scent of your deerskin
dress mingled with the smoky
smell of fire. They waltzed
leaving a transparent path of
misty tracks.

Your slippered feet touched
the ground. Shooting
electric showers of sparks
into the midnight air.

Burning holes into the curtain
of night. Sparkles speak to us
invitingly. Whispering
secrets of wonder beyond the
veil of mystery.

You danced a dance through the
night. You jumped and twisted
into the air. Leaping in
somersaults onto the tops
of trees.

You caught moonbeam arms;
swung, glided and dipped
in the midnight sky.
Talking and laughing with
your partner, the moon.

She smiled and danced to the
peak of her time. Then
retired until her next full
moon shine.

Young people had a time
trying to keep up with you.
They could no longer sit on
the outside as spectators.
The beat of the dance pulled
them in.

You egged them on, pushing
them beyond their limit.
And howled with laughter
at their attempt.

One day you were gone.
No one knows where you went.
In some ways it was as if you
were never there. Everyone
saw you, but no one really
got to know you.

Jane Inyallie

Oh, where have you gone?
Centennial Baby Doll.

Rumours were rampant. There
was much speculation as to
where you had gone. Stories
were colourful, you were seen
many places, doing many things.

Your laughter still echoes
across the lake. Playing
with water, blowing through
trees. Teasing the ears of
children.

When you left everyone missed
you. They had no one to blame.
No one to make the brunt of
their lewd joke. Then, they
realized there was more to you
than they thought.

Something was missing. The magic
and spontaneity you carried left
with you. There were a few
attempts to try and replace
it, but it never worked with
those who tried it.

The village was quiet, there
were no fiery dances on the
lake. It has been that way
since you left. The mischief
makers of the village have
grown up.

Barley's was never the same
without you. You were the
first one to get there and
the last to leave. Your
chair pushed into a corner.
No one had the courage to
sit in it.

The legacy you left has carried
to the next generation. They
stare in wonder and amazement
when stories are told of
Centennial Baby Doll.

They feel the magic of your
presence. The trickster stirs
the air with curiosity, wonder
and excitement.

Will you present yourself to
the next generation? How will
you be seen? Do people of
another time live outrageously
through you? As we did and
still do.

Oh, where have you gone?
Centennial Baby Doll.

What universe do you travel?
What dimension are you in?
What form have you taken?

Oh, where have you gone?
Centennial Baby Doll.

OHKWA:RI TA:RE TENHANONNIAHKWE
(the bear will come dance with you)

pamper below breech cloth
bustle of hawk feathers
bear shield firmly clasped in brown boy fingers
tiny braids wrapped in red felt
bear claws dangle on bone breast plate
moccasins well-worn with hole in left toe
big brown eyes drawing all into your spirit circle

mother knows the bears dance with you
the bears of your father's clan

round, round, round you go
tiny feet move to drumbeat
never seeing the crowd watching you
smiling for you
round, round, you go
following the beat of the nation drum
listening only of your spirit beat
healing those who watch with every tiny spirit step you take

in your shadow walks the eagle-- the old woman told me

sang indian songs before you talked
danced at one -- right after you walked
eagle feather presented -- you just turned two
father's pride -- mother's tears
for elder smiles you made as you danced sneak-up

you were born on Columbus day, 1990
irony of birth
day reclaimed for celebration
of you -- tiny spirit dancer

THE BLACK ONYX PALACE

Beyond waning stars
    a blue dwarf casts dim light
    upon a giant glacial world.
Beneath dark racing clouds
    frigid winds thunder
    across bleak plains of ice.
Frigid winds scream
    through dark halls
    of the Black Onyx Palace.
There
    caged-in ice
    mythical beings stand
    on black onyx floors
    heads hung in sorrow.
There
    cased in doubt
    legendary beings sit
    on grey agate thrones
    heads hung in sorrow.
There
    amid misty gloom
    and seas of salt
    beautiful beings cry
    endless tears of sorrow.

Odilia Gulvan Rodriguez

SKIN TALK

skin on skin
talking
skin on skin
beating out
the news of the day
to faraway places
skin on skin
a new ancient way
to say what's happening
then, now and tomorrow
plus
which way the four winds
are headed
today
at 5, 6 and 10
tune in

skin on skin
where life begins
a heart beat
our time piece
inside
the red womb
our new heart
with her's
beating
two
from one
inside
mother skin
taca ta
ta cata

boom boom

skin on skin
another thing
when it's color
talks too much
or not enough
about us
about who
we really are
in this skin
and even when
we say
later for that
we can't seem
to get away
from the pressure
of the skin measure

skin on skin
has always been
can be
just
the rhythm
to make things right
to shake all
the bigots out
their spigots
and down
the
drain
not to be
allowed up
the spout
again

Odilia Gulvan Rodriguez

skin on skin
rhythms to dance
the shake
the quake from
the earth
to dance back
the balance

skin on skin
to begin again in one
skin on skin
our fingers and palms
healing with feeling
our disease
will you please
our world
needs the beat

IN BEAUTY

In beauty we walk this universe,
the path of pollen is long,
In beauty we sing,
our voices-seedlings in the winds.

Judith Mountain Leaf Volborth

SONG OF INVOCATION

Ancestral voices in the wind
trailing across the night sky
whisper to me
songs of creation
and make my medicine strong.

STONES

These stones
in front of me
as they lie in this pit...

Who says they have no arms?
They reach out to me
as they hand me what I cry for.

Who says they have no eyes?
They see the innermost me
as I crouch, naked, in this lodge.

Who says they have no ears?
They hear my pitiful voice
as the sweat runs, salty, onto my tongue.

Who says they have no heart?
They love this little child
as the heat, penetrating, heals my pain.

These stones
in front of me
as they lie in this pit...

Who says they are not alive?

Jim Dumont

FASTING

I went up to a barren place
on a high hill
seeking a vision on my mind.
I saw a bearded man
hanging from a tree
and backed away.
They kill their visionaries
in this place
I thought.

I went up again to a quiet place
on a far off hill
seeking a vision still on my mind.
I saw a rich man
sitting guru-like atop a pole
and quietly left.
They sell their visions
in this place
I thought.

I went up elsewhere to a lonely place
on a desolate hill
seeking a vision foremost on my mind.
I saw a black man
suspended from a tree
and sadly turned away.
They fear their vision makers
in this place
I thought.

I went anew to an unknown place
no other tracks approached the hill
finding a vision furthest from my mind.
I saw a small tree
growing from a rock
too small to crucify a saviour
too humble for a rich man's pride
too weak to lynch a slave who dares to dream

I approached him
sat down
and waited for him
to grow.

Sandra Laronde

ANOTHER INDIGENOUS PEOPLE ACROSS THE ATLANTIC

Christmas was approaching, but instead of a familiar setting of spruce and evergreen drenched in snow, I saw ripe, abundant mango and plantain flecked with dust from a dry wind which blew from the Sahara. I remember the forest flaunting unfamiliar trees such as the cocoa, palm, niim and a sad, giant tree knowing many woes.

For nine long hours, I had been jostled around in a rickety, old lorry crammed with families, goats and fowl. When night fell, I saw the dark shapes of towering palm trees and of low bushes like great soft eagles, swooping past as we moved toward the African village where I would work as a volunteer.

I was warmly received in a farming village in the forest region of Ghana, West Africa, known as Manso-Nkwanta, which is inhabited by 120 Twi-speaking Ashanti people. I worked with both the community and a Ghanaian voluntary association to help rebuild the foundation for a primary school.

Despite the physical isolation of the village, the lack of running water and electricity, my most lasting connections were made here. I was bowled over by the incredible warmth and generosity of these people in spite of the common problems of malnourished children, lack of proper school facilities, overcrowded homes, poor roads and lack of employment.

By 4 o'clock in the morning, the village buzzed with daily activities. Women prepared meals by fire, swept the rust-hued packed earth around their homes, and tended to crying children. The men would sing in anticipation of a lorry which would take them to a nearby town (3 hours away) for work. They would leave in the darkness before dawn, and return in the evening.

In the village, the traditional division of labour exists whereby men clear and plough the land, while women cook, clean, wash and tend to children. The women also farm and this involves seed selection, harvesting, transporting crops, processing, preservation and marketing food crops. Their average work day is from 4 a.m. till 9 p.m. My next door neighbour, Akua, washed, cleaned, cared for smaller children, slaughtered fowl, attended school and did homework-all in a day's work for a 12 year old Ashanti girl. One hot day, I saw a woman walking a steady pace while carrying a 45 gallon drum on her head. I was in awe of women's physical strength and perseverance gained from hard work, not to mention their incredibly vital energy and intelligence.

On Christmas Day, the women walked in procession with keening voices throughout the village in honour of those who had recently passed into spirit. The entire day was spent in mourning.

On the following day, a great feast was prepared. The Chief poured a libation in honour of his ancestors and the Mother Earth. Then, there began a lively celebration of drumming, dancing and singing; women and men adorned in cloth of every colour. There was no exchange of material gifts in celebration of Christmas.

During my time in Manso-Nkwanta, I stayed with the very hospitable and determined "Queen Mother" known as Nana Nyarko who, like a clan mother, is well-respected by the community. She would often meet with the Elders and Chiefs, and there was always a steady stream of people requiring her attention on village matters. Indeed, she wielded considerable power in the community, yet I wondered what her position must have been before the coming of the white man. I knew that I was witnessing the diminished power of a Queen Mother.

In matrilineal societies, women held significant and highly respected political and religious positions. The Queen Mother was responsible for nominating and deposing chiefs, conducting naming ceremonies and puberty rites, marriage ceremonies and harvest festivals, etc.

I saw an old photograph of an elderly, diminutive Queen Mother named Yaa Asantewa. In 1901, when the Ashanti tradition was threatened, this 61 year old woman declared war against the British with 40,000-50,000 men under her command. The immense power of the Queen Mother, and of women's roles in general, have eroded considerably during colonial rule.

The most common drum of the Ashanti people is the "Talking Drum". This drum not only relays current messages to the community, but is also a carrier of culture. During ceremonies, people hear about their history, the battles they fought, what each family-clan is responsible for, and legends imbued with moral teachings. The Elders can still interpret the language of the talking drum, but the younger generation is losing this form of communication.

Today, instead of listening to the drum with the ancient voice, the young are moving towards Western television, radio and newspapers as their only sources of information. As they turn from the traditional drum, they lose the knowledge, wisdom and history passed on by their ancestors. Some have even forgotten their mother tongue. Many of the young have migrated to the city of Accra (9 hours away) in search of employment, formal education, and the comforts of modern, urban life.

Upon my arrival in the Ashanti village of Manso-Nkwanta, it seemed that pre-colonial traditions were still at the centre of community life. In the course of time and conversation, I began to realize that many of the ceremonies and festivals have become inextricably entwined with Christianity. However, in spite of the tremendous impact of Christianity, some Ashantis are determined to preserve their rich Indigenous tradition in the face of colonialism.

The Elders are gravely concerned with the increasing alienation of the young from Ashanti tradition. One Elder, with eyes deep and dark, told me that the younger generation in confused. They do not know who to pray to-the ancestors and traditional Gods of the Earth, or to the Christian God in heaven. While these Gods wrestle in the hearts of the young, the souls of the ancestors hunger for want of tending.

I have also heard the young say that “Times have changed”. Their future no longer lies with ancestors, living Chiefs, the Ashanti, or even the continent of Africa alone. An African writer Achebe[1] surmises: “The white is very clever. He came quietly and peaceably with his religion. We were amused at his foolishness and allowed him to stay. Now he has won our brothers and our clan can no longer act as one. He has put a knife on the things that held us together and we have fallen apart”.

From crossing the Atlantic ocean, I came to know another Indigenous people who share a similar struggle in the face of colonialism. I feel honoured to have touched the continent that gave life to these people.

Footnote:

1. Achebe, Chinva Things Fall Apart, (Heinemann Educational Books Ltd.) Nairobi, 1958

LEGEND STORY - BEN

Ben was quite old now. He hardly ever went to town anymore. He spent a lot of his time sitting on his porch, just passing time. His family were all gone. Some to different reserves to work, others away at school, still others lived in the city. Once in awhile one of his family came to visit him. He didn't seem to mind, though. He enjoyed his solitude after so much busyness. He had one particular granddaughter that he thought needed watching. She lived in the city with her mother, Ben's daughter. Jilly worked in an office. Ben wasn't sure what she did. But she was always busy. Ben saw that when they came to visit the last time.

Ben was thinking about that visit and about Fawn, when he looked up the road. Someone was turning in his driveway. He wondered who it could be. It was getting on towards supper time. He tried to make out who it was, but gave up. 'Let them get closer,' he thought. It was too hard to strain his eyes. He sat back and waited. The person slowed, then stopped a ways from the porch.

"Come a little closer," Ben said, "I can't see who it is. My eyes is not that good any more. Maybe I need glasses. I don't know." The person moved slowly toward the porch. Ben squinted, trying to make out the face. It was covered by long strands of hair. He hoped it wasn't a spook. He wasn't ready to see anyone who had gone over to the other side. He wasn't that old. All the same he got a little worried.

"Who is it?", he said a little angry now. He didn't want to let on he was worried. If they came and said it was time for him to go with him. What was he to say? He was almost ninety. Could he refuse? `Aaahh,' he thought.

He was getting old. Just like an old woman. Getting scared. He pushed himself off his chair and shuffled to the top step.

"Ooohh, it's you. Come in. How you doin'? It's good to see you. Where's you Mum? She here too? Where's the car? You walk from town?," Ben asked, holding onto the railing, trying to see Fawn's face. He stopped talking when he noticed she was crying.

"Mmmm, weell, awright. You come up here. Sit down. It's almost time to eat, you know. I can tell. The sun is just about down. In a little while I can go in and make somethin'. You hungry? I'll feed you. In a little while," Ben said, turning back to his chair. Fawn came up the steps. Her head down, wiping at her eyes and nose. Ben sat down and pulled his padded foot stool over for her to sit on. He put his arm around her and let her cry and sob as much as she wanted. After a time, when her sobs and hiccups slowed down, he began to hum a little song he remembered his own had sang to him when he was little. Funny how he still remembered it. He hummed a while, then said, "I tell you somethin', okay? A story I remember. Ohhh maybe it happened a long time ago, maybe not, I don' know. I tell you. Then we go have somethin' to eat, okay? Awright." "I heard someone tell this story a long time ago. Maybe I was small, or maybe your size. Weell, anyway... There was a young deer who didn't like how she looked. She didn't like the spots she had on her back. She didn't like her voice. She didn't like her long legs. She was very unhappy. She was sure she'd be better off if she could change just one part of her. So.. one day she run away. Just like that. She left her place. Where she live. She walked a long way. Maybe all day. She got tired and went off the trail to find a place to rest. She went under some bushes and into an open place. Not too big, small. Just a place to sit down for a while. She didn't notice Coyote sittin' there. He was feelin' kinda lazy. He never said nothin'. Kept quiet. Watched. She cry, maybe some time. Coyote got tired of hearin' her cry. So, he laugh. Loud like this. Hahaha. Hahaha. She looked, got scared. Coyote just kept laughin'.

Then, she get mad. "Don't laugh at me. I Don't even know you. You got no right to laugh at me." Coyote look at her. Then, say, "Ohh, I thought you gonna cry all day, or what's left of it. I thought I'd laugh for the rest of the day. Somethin' dif'rent anyway. Seemed like a good idea. Can't both cry all day." Little Fawn, that's her name, sat and stared at him for a while.

"I'm not goin' to cry all day. It's just that I feel bad. That's why," she say. Coyote yawns and gets up.

"Welll, since you aren't going to cry anymore, let's leave this place. I know someone up this way who might give us somethin' to eat. He's not too friendly, but I think I can get him to feed us. Let's go." They walk up the trail. OOOhh, maybe some time. Coyote went to Wolverine's house. That's where he went. Wolverine don't like comp'ny. Not much. He not too pleased to see Coyote and his comp'ny. He grunt and make angry noises and try to act mean. Maybe scare Coyote off. Coyote sit and wait for him to settle down. Then he say, "We came to visit and eat with you."

Wolverine cough and try and laugh. He don't trust that Coyote. Coyote play too many tricks on him. He don't want to feed him or his comp'ny.

"I don't have much," he says. His voice is rough and growly. "Just some real old deer meat that's just about bad. Yeah I think it has gone bad. You won't like it. No, I don't think so. No." Coyote watch him for a while. Then he say, "Well, then, tell us a story. Tell my friend how you got them short legs of yours." Wolverine glares at Coyote.

"You know how I got these short legs of mine. You were there. It was because of you I got short legs," he say, mad now. Coyote smiles and shakes his head. "You chose them. I didn't." Wolverine say, "You trick me! That's why!" Coyote say, "Well, tell us about it." Wolverine turns his back on him and looks at Little Fawn.

"At one time I had long legs. Like yours. Long strong legs. My legs are still strong, but they're short and bowed. Then, I could run very fast, so fast that your people, the deer, couldn't outrun me. I was a fast runner. A good hunter. I guess I got kinda greedy. I used to hunt just for the fun of it. Just so I could run and catch whatever I chased. I guess Coyote and others, I won't mention any names, got a little angry because I was killin' all the animals around and not eatin' 'em. They were goin' hungry. One day they decided to play a trick on me. They challenged me to a race. They said if I won I would be given even better legs to hunt with. I agreed. I was all wrap'd up in my abilities as a runner to question 'em when they said they would choose my oppon'nt. I thought it would be Coyote or one of the others. They picked Eagle. They say if I could run the same distance as Eagle could dive and reach my dest'nation the same time as Eagle's beak touched the ground, then I would be given swifter and stronger legs. I say "Okay." I lost. The penalty I receive for losin' was for them to choose new legs for me. They chose these. I went to the Creator to complain. He say I had gotten my just desserts. I was wastin' too much food and not thinkin' about others. Now, I have short legs that aren't very fast. I have to eat others' leftovers because of all the meat I wasted before. That's how Coyote tricked me out of my long legs. And, he expects me to feed him whenever he comes by, too," Wolverine finished, waddlin' to the door of his house. Coyote, he smiles to himself. He's just about to get up and move on, when they heard cacklin'.

There was Bluejay sittin' in a tree up above. "Yeah that was pretty funny. We had some fun with that old Wolverine. Yep, sure did." He laughs some more. Wolverine turns and runs at him, but he's up too high in the tree. He wouldn't be able to catch him anyway, so he says instead,"Why don't you tell this little gal how you became a winged. I bet you won't like tellin' that story," Wolverine challenges him. Bluejay stops his cacklin' and ruffles his feathers, gettin' mad.

"I'll tell it, don't you worry 'bout it. I ain't ashamed of who I am," Bluejay said, grumpy. He looks at Little Fawn, goin' to the end of the branch to see her better.

"It was like this. I used to have a diff'rent shape. Sort of like a human. I was really good lookin', real handsome. I still am. I had a real good singin' voice. Still do. I can sing. All day. Any song you wantta hear. Got any songs you watta hear? HaHa. Just kiddin'. Anyway, I was somethin' to look at. All the gals thought I was sooo good lookin'. One day I saw this little lady that was very b'yootiful. I wanted to meet her. I didn't know that Coyote was preparin' to offer a dow'ry for her. I sang her some songs. When Coyote came with his dow'ry she didn't want it. She just wanted to sit and hear me sing all day. Both her father and Coyote became angry with me. Her father, because I had turned her into a dreamer and ruined her chances of bringin' a large dow'ry to her family, and, Coyote, because she wouldn't accept him as a suitor. They thought up a plan to change my looks so I wouldn't be so good lookin'. They told me that there were some times and places that I couldn't sing. In my ar'gance I said no, I could sing at any time and place they chose. They chose Salmon's house. I couldn't sing underwater. They won and chose this body for me. I complained, of course, to the Creator. But he said I should have accepted my own lim'tations and not been so determined to be right. Now, I have to sit in the treetops all day and sing my songs, because I bragged of being able to sing anywhere and anytime." Bluejay finishes and flies to the treetop and sings loud again. Coyote is about to get up, again, when this chatterin' stops him. He turns and sees Chipmunk sittin' at the edge of the clearin'.

"I want to tell my story. I have a story to tell. I need to tell my story. I want you to hear my story, Little Fawn," Chipmunk chatters. Coyote moans and groans and sits down again. "So tell it," he says. Impatient, you know. Chipmunk starts.

"I used to be dif'rent, real dif'rent, kinda dif'rent, really very dif'rent. I was bigger, larger, huge. Welll, not that big. A little big. Maybe not so big, but not small either. Well not really small. Just a little bigger than not so small. Welll maybe not that small. Not that big either. Anyway, I was not always this size. I had a very nice coat. Nice and soft, fluffy, warm. Not as fluffy as a rabbit's tail, not that fluffy, but fluffy. Maybe not fluffy, but smooth and sleek. Like an otter. No, not really. More like halfway between fluffy and sleek. But nice. Very nice. I was proud of my coat. I liked to show my coat to ev'ryone. Ev'ryone who would listen. I would walk around and show my coat to ev'ryone. I thought it was the best. I guess one day ev'ryone got tired of me showin' them my coat. Coyote, and some others got together to trick me out of my coat so they wouldn't have to listen to me anymore. I guess I was not much comp'ny. I was comp'ny, but not good comp'ny. I had comp'ny, but I didn't. My comp'ny wasn't comp'ny if I didn't make them feel like comp'ny. You know what I mean? Anyway, they got together and made a plan to steal my coat from me. I walked into town one day, holdin' my coat to the side and showin' it to anyone who wanted to see. Not very many did. See I mean. I mean wanted to see. They saw, but they didn't want to see. They had all saw it all before. Anyway, I walked along. Coyote came up to me and says, "You're coat isn't as nice as Skunk's. No. Not as nice." I got angry. Of course I had seen Skunk's coat. It was nice, but I didn't like it. Not as much as I liked my own. It wasn't that I didn't like Skunk's coat. It was that I didn't like someone likin' Skunk's coat better than mine. I got angry. I say, "If I tried on Skunk's coat, it would look better on me than on him. I can make any coat look good on me. If I traded Skunk coats, I would still have the best coat. It's the wearer not the coat." Coyote, he challenge me. He say, "Well why not try on Skunk's coat and see if it looks better on you than on him?" I said "Okay, give it here." Skunk took off his coat and gave it to me. I put it on. Since Skunk was smaller than me, I had to squeeze it on. I didn't know that they had put some pitch inside the coat to make it stick. I struggled and struggled and tried to get the coat off. I couldn't. The more I struggled the more it stuck. I pulled and twisted and turned, this way and that. Pretty soon I was all in knots. I couldn't move. Coyote say, "If I help, will you stop braggin' about your coat. I said, "Yes." He say, "The coat is too tight and too small to get off. We're going to have to make you smaller to get it off. That's the only way. So, I was made smaller by one of Coyote's tricks. They were able to get most of the coat off, except for two dark stripes down my back. That's why I have dark stripes and Skunk has white stripes. My coat was pure white at one time and Skunk's was black. That's my story. Well not my whole story. Just a part of my story. A small part. There's lots more..." Coyote, he jumps up and pulls Little Fawn behind him.

"Let's go before he gets started again," he says. Little Fawn says, "Why'd they tell me all these stories?" Coyote didn't say anythin' for a time. Then, he say, "Maybe you needed to hear them. I don't know. What do you think? Myself, I don't know." Coyote sits on a stump and watches Little Fawn. Little Fawn thinks for a while. "I'm not sure, Maybe. I think I have to think about it for a while," she say, thinkin'. "Coyote, do you think I have a nice coat, and a nice voice and my legs aren't too long?"

Coyote, he sit and think. "Yep, they're right for you. For who you are. Do you know who you are? What you're supposed to be? See, ev'ryone has a place in this world. Ev'ryone has their own looks. Now, if you use that place or those looks against people or for your own self, then, that's no good. Wolverine got too greedy and wanted more than what he alr'edy had. That's no good. Be satisfied with what you got. Bluejay was too caught up in what he was. That's no good either. Be satisfied with what you got, but too much is too much. There's a middle ground we have to walk. Don't worry people about what you do have. It gets tir'some. Like Chipmunk. You may have to set'le for less, like he did. It's good to like yourself, but not to excess. That's not to say you should hate yourself. That's no good either. Be willin' to see what you're good at and work at those. Don't worry about what you can and can't do. It's no good to compare yourself to others. Be yourself. That's how the Creator made you. Just the way you are. Work with what he gave you. If he's satisfied with you, who are you to be unsatisfied. If you want to change what he made, you might get into trouble like Wolverine and Bluejay and Chipmunk. You have to walk the road the Creator set for you to walk. What do you think? You think that's why you heard those stories today? Me, I don't know. Let's go. I need to find somethin' to eat. I'm hungry." Coyote walks off up the trail. And, that's the story."

"Now, you ready to eat? I think I can rustle som'thin' up," Ben said, looking at Fawn. She was thinking. He got up and went into the house to build up the fire. Fawn sat there for a while, then she went into the house after Ben.

"Grandpa, how come you always know what stories to tell me? You always pick stories that make me feel better. I'm glad you know so much stories. I need to hear them now and again," Fawn said, sitting at the table. Ben smiled to himself. `Yep, this little girl was special,' he thought. It was good she come home to him. She needed to get out of the city once in a while. They can go down the road after supper and call her Mum. Maybe, her Mum will come and stay for a while too. She needed to hear stories too. Ben decided that maybe he better make supper for three. Jilly will be hungry when she gets here. She was already on her way.

DARKNESS IS MY SILENCE

I was sitting in the darkness
when the light came to my doorway
And I spent my time just watching
from one darkness to another
As the light played out my resistance
and it pushed back on the sadness
I thought: this light will be my beacon
for the journey I am to follow
But it had no way to lead me
since light is only known to darkness
So I sat there as day slipped back into night.

The baby slept there in the silence
when a thoughtsound touched his heartbeat
And he waited for the morning
listening to the waves that pounded
As his spirit called for him to waken
and gave purpose to the dreaming
He thought: I will look for the doorway
that will lead me to the daylight
But there was no one to lead him
since the light only shone inside him
So he turned around and slipped out of the night

Jim Dumont

The darkness was my beginning
when the flesh thundered its arrival
And I listened as it came nearer
from one darkness to another
As the throbbing filled the vastness
and it pushed back the walls of reason
I thought: the darkness is my silence
and the light is there inside me
So there is no one to lead me
since the light gives shape to darkness
So I walked on down the shining path of night.

BLUE AGAINST WHITE

Lena walked up the steep hill toward her mothers's house. She could see the bright blue door. It stood out against the stark white of the house. It was the only house with a door like that on the hill. All the houses on that part of the reserve looked a lot alike, the colours ranging from mostly white to off-white to grey, and a few with light pastel colours. All the doors matched the houses.

Thinking of it now, Lena realized that it was funny how she had always thought of it as her mother's house rather than her father's house, though it had been his idea to paint the door a bright blue. He had said that the houses up there on the hill all looked too much alike. He had said that their home would be easy to see because of the door. He was right, but there was a question that had always been silent: "Who would have a problem?" She had known that all the Indians in a thousand-mile radius knew each other and that they didn't find their way to each other by the description of their houses.

As she walked toward the house she realized that she had kept that door in her mind all the years she had been away. It has been there as always, a bright blue against the white. A blue barrier against the cold north wind. A cool blue shield against the summer heat. She remembered having hated the door and having wished it would just be white like the rest of the house. But while she was away, it had been the part of the house that had been a constant clear image. Behind that door, warm smells and laughter mixed into a distinct impression of the way it was back home. Her mother, long braids tied together in the back, smiled at her from behind that door.

Now, she walked up the hill toward the house carrying the one bag that held her things. She felt light, weightless and somehow insubstantial like the last fluffseeds still clinging shakily to the milkweeds that lined the narrow dirt road gutted with deep, dry ruts. In this country the summer rains left cracked mud tracks which froze in the fall and stayed hidden under the snow and ice in winter.

At this moment she felt she could easily be lifted to float up and away from those deep earth gashes, to move across the land with the dry fall drifting of seeds and leaves. She had hated this dirt road and the mud in the spring and the dust in the summer, the ruts in the fall and the ungraded snow in the winter. She had mostly hated the dry milkweeds crowding together everywhere. As always, on this road the lumps of soil were uneven and slow to travel over. She felt like turning and bolting back to the bus to catch it before it could leave her here, but running was hard on this broken ground.

The door seemed to loom ahead of her, though the house was no taller than the rest. She hated the way all the cheap government houses on the row facing the road were so close together and had paint peeling and dry weedy yards with several mangy dogs. She turned to look back at the road winding steeply down to the cross-road where the bus stopped momentarily to drop off or pick up people from the reserve. The freeway stretched away into a hazy purple distance where night was beginning to shadow the land. Only the white line dividing those coming from those going was visible after a certain point. The red lights of the bus were fading straight into that shadow line between sky, asphalt and the darkened earth.

Turning, she faced the rest of the climb. A single black crow cawed at her from its perch on the steeple cross of the village church, raising a raucous in the quiet. It screeched and flapped its wings, dove over her mother's house and then flew lazily overhead, looking down at her as it passed, flying over the dirt road toward the crossroad in the direction of the twilight.

She watched the crow disappear into dark blue. She knew his name from the old stories. She wanted to laugh and say it. She knew he hung around only in the summer months and then flew away when the shadows in the fall grew long and the days short. She wanted to say, "You, old pretender, you don't fool me. You're not going to preach to me, too, are you? You're no smarter than me!" Instead she found tears wetting her cheeks.

Her tears brought the memory of a dream from the week before she had started the long bus ride home. In her dream she had been in a large building with many bright lights and shiny reflections. Although there was a lot of noise, she couldn't see anyone. She felt totally alone as she walked down a long white hallway. She remembered looking, one by one, at the doors she passed, feeling like the only thing behind each one was a patch of sky. In the dream she remembered feeling something like dizziness as she saw how many doors there were and how they seemed to stretch into darkness on and on without end. She recalled running and stumbling past the doors and calling out. When she awoke she had been crying.

She was almost at the top of the hill now. She stopped and put down her bag. A couple of reserve dogs barked at her and then wagged their tails, trotting toward her, making greeting noises in their throats. She looked down at the one that was obviously a lady dog with her sagging dry milk sacs and she stroked her ear. She thought of the city she had left and said, "Mamma dogs don't just walk around free there, you know. You're pretty lucky to be here." The lady dog sat down and thumped her tail against some of the weeds, sending puffs of seed floating with each excited wave.

Behind the houses farther up into the dark hills, she heard the high, far-away yipping of a coyote. She saw the dogs' ears perk up. She saw the way their eyes glowed a deeper orange as they forgot her and pointed their noses toward the hills above them, a low, crooning echo rumbling deep in their throats. She, too, looked up there and whispered, "How are you, brothers?" in the language. She knew them, too.

She thought of that one coyote in the papers, in some city, that had got trapped in a hallway after coming in from an alley door. How somebody mistaking it for a dog had opened an elevator for it and how it had ridden to the roof of an apartment building and ran around crazily, and then jumped to its death rather than run back through the elevator door and ride back down into the hallway and out the alley door. She had known that it hadn't been a matter of animal stupidity, because a coyote always remembered where it had come from. She had secretly known that it had more to do with the quick elevator door and the long lonely ride up to the top. She thought of the coyotes hanging around in the cities these days. Nobody wanted them there, so nobody made friends with them, but once in a while they made the papers when they did something wrong or showed up, trotting along Broadway, cool as could be.

Lena thought about all the time she had spent away from this place of hard, cracked earth, seedpods and clean coyote prints in the new snow up in the hills. She looked up at the bright blue surface directly in front of her, waiting to open, and felt the bone-aching, deep tiredness of long journeys over the hard even surface of freeways into alleys and white hallways. As she reached for the door knob she looked down and realized that the freeway's white line and the mud ruts ended here, right at her mother's door. The door that her dad had painted bright blue so that it stood out clearly against the white.

CIRCLE THE WAGONS

there it is again, the circle, that goddamned circle, as if we thought in circles, judged things on the merit of their circularity, as if all we ate was bologna and bannock and lived in teepees, drank Tetley tea, so many times "we are" the circle, the medicine wheel, the moon, the womb, and sacred hoops, you'd think we were one big tribe, is there nothing more than the circle in the deep structure of native literature? Are my eyes circles yet? Yet I feel compelled to incorporate something circular into the text or the plot, narrative structure because if its linear then that proves that I'm a ghost and that native culture really has vanished and what is all this fuss about appropriation anyway? Are my eyes round yet? There are times when I feel that if I don't have a circle or number four or legend in my poetry, I am lost, just a fading urban Indian caught in all the trappings of doc martens, cappuccinos and foreign films but there it is again orbiting, lunar, hoops encompassing your thoughts and canonizing mine, there it is again, circle the wagons....

SOCIETY

THE GRACEFUL AWAKENING

George had quite a content life as a young man. He'd fathered two boys, as well as a daughter. But when he learned that his wife of fifteen years had been seeing a well-established businessman, he began living his life through a wine bottle, in a very distinguished way at first.

Hoping that the affair was just a phase his wife was going through, he tried to ignore the situation. As he'd done in the beginning of their relationship, he started wining and dining her again. However, there was no romance left on her part. He eventually gave up courting her and would get drunk whenever they went out to dinner. When he could get nowhere with his romantic attempts, he started slapping her around. She would not take such physical abuse and had him removed from their home, which he had worked for so many years to provide for his family.

Two years later, when the divorce was final, George was living in a run-down hotel room, in the skid row part of town. Through drinking and gambling, he'd lost his job and ended up on welfare.

The first time his children snuck away from home to visit him he felt his eyes water, but then he became angry and told them never to set foot in that part of town again. By then their mother had remarried. He told his teenage children their stepfather could do more for them than he ever could, so it'd be best for them to just forget him. To convince them how serious he was, he offered them a drink of wine from his gallon, but not too much 'cause it had to last him a couple of days. He could see them wiping their tears away as the three of them boarded the bus. He never saw or heard from them again.

On his straight days, George often reminisced with his park bench buddies about his young days. Like the times he went hunting with his brothers.

"Them were the days," he'd say, before he got started on one of his hunting stories.

"One time, when me and the boys went hunting, we were walking along this dirt road along the way to the river in Westholme, such a beautiful sight. It was very early in the morning, and it was raining quite heavily. There was a little stream just before we got to the river; the fish were spawning around that time, so we stopped to watch them fighting the rapids. I never saw so many baldheaded eagles in all my life. A couple of them buzzards went swooping down to snatch their prey, while another half-dozen were perched in them centuries old fir trees. We could even see more of 'em flyin' high up in the sky, like they were playing games with each other. From that day on, I often wondered just what it would be like to feel as free as them beautiful birds. To be able to observe the world from above."

As time went on, George ended up living right on skid row. He was well known in this part of town as a harmless panhandler. Quite the penny pinching panhandler too. For, at the end of the each day, he'd put his change in a tin container with a lid, and bury it in an alley, which his wino friends seemed to overlook. Each time his container was full he'd put on his Sunday best suit, which he chose from a Goodwill box in the more sophisticated part of town, and off to the bank he'd go, deposit his hard-earned coins, and start all over. Even the children of the community gave him their spare change; and when they needed change themselves, George would return the favor.

Over the years, George's bank account grew larger and larger. He never spent a penny of it on himself, other than to buy his gallon of wine once or twice a week. He arranged to have his savings split among his three children after his passing. Knowing that they would be all right, George decided he would follow his lifelong dream: he would return to the river where he'd seen all those beautiful eagles. The time was right, and George was happy that he would be able to relive a day in his past that had given him his dream.

When he finally arrived at the river, it was as if he had never left. He sat on the riverbank with his wine beside him, and talked to the eagles as if they were his friends. And they squawked right back at him as though he understood everything they were squawking about.

Human society came to the conclusion that George had died from alcoholism. Truth was, George hadn't died at all: his spirit had left the human body and had entered the eagle he had become closest to.

Duncan McCue

WINDIGO SMILE

At night we walked.
Packs
walking the village
with bottles.

When snowmobiles whined,
        we thought of
                the Windigo scream.
We went home for tea.

The Windigo, noshomis said,
ate 'Nishnawbe. He take
away the Spirit from your body,
freeze you solid - paralysed.
Then he eat you.

Don't stay out late -
        you meet the Windigo.

I was at the Airport this morning,
bumped into a smiling DIA man
on his way to our conference.

There was the sound of jets
whining in my ears.

CHILD STANDING ALONE

a cry breaks from the little girl's throat,
as her mother and father say
"good-bye, we won't be long".
and there is a
child standing alone
in a two room home.

the mother reaches down to touch
her daughter, but her hand stops short.
the child stops the cry,
and fists at her side
she turns away.
and there is a
child standing alone
staring at the walls
of a two room home.

the father at the door yells
at his wife. "hurry up, it's near closin' time".
they leave and bitter voices
can be heard behind the closed door.
and there is a
child standing alone,
locking the door
to her two room home.

the daughter cries, now a woman
with children of her own.
please take time to listen.
she needs that two room home
for she is a
child standing alone.

T. Marshall

UNTITLED

How many times since your legislated lies
will too many red children want to lay down and die.
They've followed your white ways
and bought all your wrongs
of deliverance, integrity,
justice and pride.

Somewhere in time, exiled in haste
the sweepers of discovery
spit in their face.
They cut off their noses, their culture, their faith
and changed them to tokens,
the Indian race.

Where are we going and who's in this race
toward exile and hatred,
walkers in the waste.
Whose gonna get there and whose gonna cry
for the culture in mourning
whose children have died.

Borrow your own lies,
sell them, their cheap.
Bank them, borrow them,
the interest is steep.

Hang out your own sighs,
we'll iron them for cheap
and use them for bedsheets
for the children that sleep.

Borrow your own truth,
we'll wrap it in stride
and use it to mirror
your cultural lies.

We'll cut them and paste them
to the coffin of why's
that rise up from the earth
for the children that cry.

The lies can be aired then
and mended and tied,
to the train of deliverance,
recapturing our pride.

HE CROW AND HIS BRAGGING

He crow and She crow were sitting on a great cottonwood tree enjoying a warm sunny day. It was a beautiful afternoon, with the autumn leaves rustling and the fresh smell of Indian summer coming on.

"Such a nice day" Yawned She crow.

"That it is" Replied He crow.

"I am feeling especially great today."

He crow fluffed his feathers and strutted the length of the cottonwood's massive branch. Suddenly, a great bald eagle came into view, gliding over the horizon on the wind's updraft.

"Oh my." Said She crow. "It's Mr. eagle."

"He must be out hunting, searching for prey," He crow jealously exclaimed, once again puffing up his feathers.

"He looks so fierce and strong. We better not make too much noise," She crow meekly whispered.

"Oh horse feathers," He crow angrily retorted.

"I am just as strong as your so called 'Mr. eagle,' and just as good of a hunter also. After he's gone I will show you, just wait and see."

He crow then hopped madly to the far end of the branch.

After Mr. eagle passed overhead and was just a speck in the distance. He crow strutted to the edge of the limb and with a great leap of arrogance swooped off into the air. He climbed the upper air drafts higher and higher, until he was as high as Mr. eagle had been. When he reached the peak of his climb, he slowly began his descent, spiraling down in wild circles, scanning the praire below.

Suddenly he spotted a small field mouse humbly foraging through the tall grass. He crow made a quick glance towards the cottonwood tree, so as to assure himself that she crow was watching, and began his dive. Faster and faster, his arrow-like descent became. The mouse was in target and He crow gleefully thought, "Now I will show her".

Just as he honed in for the finishing strike, the humble little mouse, seeing the oncoming shadow, darted into the nearby secret hole designed just for such occasions and disappeared into the safety of the ground.

He crow's dive was too fast, with sudden horror he tried to put on the brakes, but in his enthusiasm to impress had overdone his speed. All he could do was to close his eyes in regret.

From She crow's vantage point, He crow's dive was incredible, and for a moment she thought he somewhat resembled Mr. eagle, but just for that moment. The explosion and small puff of dirt and dust that billowed up in the air scared the blackbirds that were watching and sent them flying in all directions. After the small cloud of dust had been blown away and the blackbirds had settled down once again, quieting their squawking, She crow gently hopped off the branch and flew over to investigate. What she saw made her feathers shake in surprise. A hole in the ground and nothing else, at least that is what she tells her friends.

Sitting under the shade of the large cottonwood tree, now green with summer, She crow can be seen cawing in gossip with her friends and young ones. Talking about the brave deeds of He crow and how he was so great a hunter he chased a mouse into the bowels of the earth, and was to this day, still chasing it far below.

MEDICINE WORDS

kind warriors
gentle warriors
warriors of song & dance
warriors of words & wisdom
warriors free, imprisoned
warriors of words
        honest & daring & caring & hopeful
words clear, present, transcending
reflecting images of life & our heart's wishes
words for tomorrow & words for us now
words for the young ones & words for the old

warriors in spirit

today our weapons are words
like arrows, many arrows
piercing & penetrating
        hearts, eardrums
leaving arrowheads, messages buried deep
deep in the souls of those mean spirits
        spirits which still haunt this land

arrowheads dipped in medicine
weapons of love, when love can't always be kind
medicine wings
medicine arrows
healing wounds, recovering fully
returning to the circle
returning to the circle
ready for more words
ready to listen
and love

mean spirits a memory
nightmare
spirits healed by our medicine words
our circle always growing
our voices like the ocean waves, rising and falling
our breath like the wind, constant & unending
carrying messages, medicine words
from the spirits within
the spirit of our mothers, grandmothers
spirits alive still

our words a song unbroken & strong
many echoes, many memories, many voices
together calling---

return to the circle when you are ready
my friend

IN THE SUNSHINE OF THIS NIGHT

this evening is a cool one
like so many lately
and the moon is full
her light shining down and touching the earth
our bodies warming
our skin glowing
in the sunshine of this night

tonight
while this light shines bright
burning a path into tomorrow, awakening a new dawn
we wait, anticipating changes
and hoping that happiness will not be lost
as it often is when wars never end
and tensions take their toll
on we so innocent and unknowing how to end the war
the wars
knowing all too easily how to create bloody corpses
but forgetting how to heal

heal these wounds today
heal these open gashes
heal today before tomorrow's wars begin
and the full moon shining becomes a target passing
unable to evade the guns of men angry
existing only to shine until all candlelight has melted
and the fires of human need have burnt out
tired of struggle
tired of war
we are the people who are tired of fighting
wanting to feel the moonlight's warmth without
fear of attack

wanting to believe that sharing life is possible
and war will end soon
and wanting to pursue a promise of peace
for so long so felt in our hearts
today, tonight
i remember world wars
indian wars
the genocide and decimation

but i am not afraid
i do not fear those angry
i am a fighter
and will raise my hands against your lightning
you cannot silence me, nor destroy me
with words of hate and angry glares

i am a fighter
remembering...

when memory was but a rainbow
and a vision for world peace.

TWO ACT POEM

Act 1

My people
It was so long ago
That I called you by
that collective name.
Now I am wiser.
You speak the language
Of those who cut out your tongues;
You wear the clothes
Of those who raped you;
You drive into your coffins
the nails that they invented.
My heart weeps blood
For those
Who danced for strength,
Whose shadows still dance
On this earth.
Where are these people now,
Those people?
Sometimes
I catch a glimpse
Of my ancestors
In the eyes of those
on Skid Row.
They know,
But
They don't
Fight anymore.
And from time to time
The eyes of a "successful"

Indian
Cry out with pain
Of what they've misplaced.
Oh
They know all...
But it was lost
Dust in the wind,
Long before
They
Came into this world.
Yes,
My heart weeps blood
For those
Who danced for strength
Whose shadows still dance
On this earth.

Act II

I fell into the cracks
of the sidewalk
And
Lay there
With the
Fingers of dust.
But
Cold North-Wind
Blew me back to Earth.
Raging,
Sweating blood,
I
Felt
Myself slip and trip,
Not wanting to
Get up

But
Finding myself
On my feet
each time.
Each time, avoiding mirrrors
Running
But
Still
outside in inside out
I
can't get away.

Screaming
I'm screaming
Glass
Shatters and
cracks
Eagles cry
clouds weep
But
Nobody hears.
Family
Friends
Touch me
Tell me
what and
where and why-
What
new kind am I
Where
do we meet
and Why
is there no
reflection of me...

Valerie Dudoward

Grandfather,
I
need a friend,
Let's share secrets
That
Only we
can keep;
I
Love
your stories
and
Happy songs;
We'll
sing
When
I visit you.

And
you'll say,
Just
Like
you always used to,
That
My birth was meant
to be
and My time
is now And...
Grandfather.
I'll visit you
Soon,
Under your
Cool stone house
In the hidden village.

BIRTHMARK

(FOR TREVOR EVANS)

I remember the panic on my younger brother's face, Roger, when he saw my scars. He came back to town from College for Christmas break. "Jesus, Rich, what happened?" he asked. I could have told him the truth but I told him it was a birthmark.

"But you weren't born with it," He said. "Tell me the truth. How did it happen?"

"It's just like Dr. Hoffman said," I answered. "Sometimes birthmarks come to you later on in life. Sometimes people get them when they're in their thirties, sometimes in their forties."

"Well can't they give you something for it?"

"Sure. They could give me acid and burn it off, or they can use a sander and obliterate the skin leaving a bigger scar".

He winced. "Man that would hurt."

"Exactly".

"So what are you gonna do? It looks like a hickey or something".

"Well it was first diagnosed as skin cancer and then..."

"Cancer!"

"Yeah, skin cancer," I emphasized. "and then it was diagnosed as juvenile warts."

"Well whatchagonna do?" he asked.

"Don't know". I answered. I could tell he was disgusted with my scar, so I started to tease. "It changes shape! It changes color!"

"Hey!" My brother threw his hands at me and walked away.

"It's alive!" I teased and started to giggle-- something I've been guilty of even as a child. I could never keep a straight face in the darkest moments: Indian humor I'm told.

He shot around as if to stop the game in its tracks. "We'll kill it, Richard, Just kill it."

I stood there long after he had gone into the house and I ran my finger over the coarse skin. It felt like something scaly, something warm and scaly that had burrowed in my neck, leaving its husk exposed for all to stare at. The scar itself is located at the base of my neck, above the collar bone.

"Just kill it."

I wish I could.

I guess a long time ago, when Fort Smith used to be a boom town during World War Two, there was this gentleman named Mr. Twisted Finger. He rented out his house to the best poker players in the Northwest Territories. His house was smack dab in the middle of Indian Village. Nobody got into any scraps in his house because everyone respected him. It was not uncommon for the games to last for days. Sometimes players would get so feverish in their game, they would throw their truck keys on the table or a pair of moccasins or a moose-hide jacket or their best pair of shit-kickers. Mr. Twisted Finger watched on, making his money from an entrance fee, and his six daughters, who were rumored to be the best cooks in town, would sell stew and bannock-- even in the throws of a good game the players would sometimes call "time-out" and share a meal. Like I said, it was a good time and a lot of people made some good money in that house, however; a lot of hard working trappers lost a season's worth of furs in a few hours. There was no drinking allowed in Mr. Twisted Finger's house, and that was just fine with everyone who came to play.

Well I guess one night there was a knock on the door, it was a Friday, payday. Mr. Twisted Finger opened the door and saw a tall stranger waiting for him out in the yard. It was winter out and the stranger was all dressed in black. He wore gloves and had long hair. He could have been a Half-breed, sometimes it's hard to tell. The stranger made no move to come into the house until invited, and even then he didn't speak.

Mr. Twisted Finger barred him before he went into the house and said, "Buddy, that'll be four dollars to play in my house."

Mr. Twisted Finger used to be one of best trappers in the South Slave area but he wrecked his knees one year by having a tree buck on him when it fell. He told the men after that night that when the stranger gave him the money, and when his hands touched the stranger's glove all that stiffness he had been feeling went away. It was like someone breathed a puff of warm air in his knees and he walked the stranger into his house with his arm wrapped around him.

"Gentlemen!" he called out, "this here stranger's gonna join you at the poker table, so make him comfortable."

As he was saying this, I guess, everybody smelt something mighty high, like out-house shit on a hot humid day. Everybody covered their noses and asked Mr. Twisted Finger if it was a good idea to let the stranger into the house. Mr. Twisted Finger said he couldn't smell anything, and when the stranger pulled out a wad of cash as big as his fist nobody seemed to be able to smell anything either.

They played what was called "bullshit poker". I don't know if you know what that is and I don't either, but that's what they used to play, and right away that stranger started to lose. Everybody tried to talk to him, as that was the custom. They wanted to know where he was from, if he was in the army, if he was a drifter trying to make a little money, or if he was related to anyone in town. They were just being polite-- no harm in that -- especially if you're taking all his money! but he couldn't answer; and all through the games, he kept his long black jacket on, and his gloves too.

All five of Mr. Twisted Finger's girls were hovering around the handsome stranger hoping to catch his eye. They offered him stew and bannock, but I guess he was a mute, couldn't speak. That was fine enough and he was losing-- which makes it finer still, he can't complain-- and he lost and lost. Finally, after about eight straight hours and a lot of money circulating that table, the stranger was broke. Mr. Twisted Finger had been watching him all night and put his hand on the stranger's shoulder to bid him a polite farewell, but when he touched the stranger's long black coat he said it was like someone blew ice in his knees.

"Sir," he said as he winced, "I'm going to have to ask you to leave. There's about three guys here who want to take your seat at the table".

The stranger calmly stood up and began to smile. He bent over the table and shook everybody's hand and started to laugh-- I mean he started to laugh really loud, and I guess the men who had taken all of his money smiled and laughed with him. Soon everyone started to get a little scared. They hadn't heard anything from him the whole night, and here he was laughing right in their faces!

After he shook their hands, he started to walk out of the house, and one of the girls who was just finished making a fresh pot of stew came in from the kitchen and said good night to him, but as she did, she dropped her pot all over the floor and called out, "Look."

Everybody stood up and rushed over, and from under the stranger's coat, before he went out the door, dragged a cow's tail.

Everybody in the house recoiled and the stranger started to laugh again as everybody threw the still warm money back on the table.

But it was too late, I guess. The deal was made.

The next day they could see that in the tracks of the stranger's cowboy boots, there were holes cut into the feet right where the toes should have been and in those tracks were hooves.

Well that there story was told to me by Red Kettle Woman, as they called her. She told this to me before she passed away.

But I didn't want to hear that story. I didn't even know anything about Mr. Twisted Finger's house-- that was before I was born. I had wanted to know about her scar, the one that I kept seeing everytime her scarf slipped or loosened as she was getting into the Handi-Bus for bingo. I'm the town driver. Anyways, I kept asking her and asking her, "Red Kettle Woman, could you tell me how you got them scars?" She kept telling me I didn't want to know.

I would bring her gifts: silver spoons for her collection, Labrador tea, or Kinniknick leaves which she liked to smoke. I brought her lots of stuff, just for that story, and then she told me.

She told me about Mr. Twisted Finger's house and poker games. I guess one night, one of Mr. Twisted Finger's girls was really sick and he hired her for the night because it was a payday and he knew it would be a mighty busy-- that's when people felt the luckiest-- and that girl that seen the tail, that was Red Kettle Woman who seen it and pointed it out.

She said when she dropped the stew, some of it splashed her body and that's how she got those scars.

Funny thing though, the day she died, which was Mother's Day, 1991, that was the day I got my scar. At first I ignored it, but then people started to ask about it when I'd go swimming down at the rapids, or if I'd take off my shirt when I was tarring roofs for Johnny Vogt. I just tell them I got kissed by the devil-- that shuts them up and it's better that I don't tell them the truth. I ain't never gonna tell this story to anyone, not even my younger brother. I don't want to give anyone what I got, and it's better that part of Fort Smith's history die with me.

Nope, I ain't gonna tell this story to no one. Ever...

William George

STORMS TO FLY THROUGH

Life
flight of eagles
we are not born to fly
attempt fail attempt learn
each time we gain confidence
storms line our course
storms cloud our way
air currents take us down
we endure through
hurting healing adapting
in our daily flights
emotions plummet or soar
we learn to soar through storms

Person
a cocoon and butterfly
caterpillar goes through metamorphosis
emerges butterfly
self-image cocoon
self-image needs nurturing
expresses butterfly to the world
butterfly contains everything a person has
everything a person is

Person lays dormant
person emerges
expresses butterfly
soars through storms
person continues on

OLD RUBY IN THE PARK

Old Ruby, sitting in the park.
You're more noticeable, because your skin is dark.
Although you've done no wrong,
The rookie policeman tells you to move along.
A group of punks sit nearby,
smoking a "J" to get high.
The rookie turns a blind eye and just saunters on by.

Old Ruby what happened to you?
Did you believe? - Did you really believe what they said
about Indians is true?

I notice hairs of grey as she hobbles on her way.
"God," I pray, "Don't let me end up like that some day".

Will I be strong enough to survive?
When I'm her age - will I even be alive?
I'm still chasing my dreams.
Unnoticed, the tears trickle down like a miniature stream.
It's not humanly fair - we were here first,
yet, we are treated the worst.

Oh well!, time to straighten the tie and shirt.
Time to tuck back the hurt.
Lunch break is finished and I feel so diminished.

Walking, sipping on my Coke, I notice the punks are
wailing on old Ruby with a drunk Indian joke.
Casually, as I walk by, some Coke will accidently fly.
SPLASH!, Geez, it hits three or four and their mouths say
no more. At six foot five, that's probably the only reason
I'm still alive.

Suddenly, I feel my quest IS worthwhile and I head back to work with a great big smile.

Old Ruby what happened to you?
Did you believe? - Did you really believe what they said about Indians is true?

DREAMING TOGETHER

Remember
last night
in the moonlight
when silver moonbeams re
fract
ed
through crystal window panes
when amidst a s
p
e
c
t
r
u
m

a winged horse appeared
when in silence
we flew!

Pamela GreenLaBorge

THE WEB AND THE WASTE LAND

For T.S. Eliot.

(Note: Grandmother Spider/Spider Woman/Thought Woman is a Pueblo Indian concept. All stories and thoughts originate from her; she functions as the primal source for all thoughts.)

Thomas Stearns Eliot
Never knew
Grandmother Spider.
Because if he did,
He'd have known
The Waste Land was
A state of mind.

He'd have known,
The Spider
Was feeding him
Strands.
Long iridescent
Threads of thought
Spun deep
Within her shadow.

If he looked closer
In some crevice
Of his rock,
He would have seen her.
Spinning,
Connecting,
Joining.

Mapping.
All four directions,
Into circle.
Into wholeness
Into meaning.
Across generations
And cultures.

T.S., never knew
About Grandmother Spider.
Because if he did,
He would have stayed
Right here.
In North America,
And talked with her.
She would have
Showed him,
Where to look
For life and peace.
No need to travel
Continents.
Collecting fragments.

THE MOUNTAIN LION - CLOSE ENCOUNTERS

Despite near perfect weather conditions for deer hunting, the long day proved to be uneventful. Temperatures hovered around freezing points, depending on the altitude. I was working the southwest ridge of Mount Evans, moving up, down and across. The air was nippy, with a Jack Frost bite, and the snow was wet, just the kind for making snowmen. I was stalking prey, searching in and out of the altitudes. A few deer had moved up too far ahead and I was unable to get a kill shot off. In this area the earth sharply inclines in between ravines. Visual sighting is brief and limited. If one is careful you can hear the deer snort as they rise to run, or you can smell them if the wind is right and if your urban senses are accustomed to the wild.

Usually it takes about three or four days in the forest, before my senses clear and I can see what I'm supposed to see, and smell what I'm supposed to smell. It takes time to hear the distinct sounds, other than the wind and running brooks.

I had been hunting alone since before daylight and had not seen another hunter in this vast area of wilderness, assuring me I was quite alone. The area is so large and rough a thousand hunters would not likely run into each other.

The day was partly sunny, with some overcast skies. I noticed when the sun finally broke out I only had an hour or more of daylight. It was time to start heading back down toward my parked truck. The truck was down a trail about three and a half miles back deep in the forest. I went back as far as I dared go with my vehicle, as it was not a four-wheeler. In case of a sudden snow storm, I had parked facing the road. It was tricky, for the narrow trail wedged my truck on both ends, and I had to bully a small bush to get it turned around.

As I headed back down, I picked a ravine, or wash out to be my trail. These waterways serve as a guide down the steep slopes, as they run into larger brooks or streams further below. As well, their rock bases are a natural stepping stone, acting like stairs downward. It is easier to go down some very steep inclines and rough country. As a hunter, the banks on both sides serve to conceal movement. The sound of running water falling downward eliminates any sounds you might make - breaking of a twig or the kicking of loose stones. The confinement between the banks of the watershed tends to confine your smell or scent.

I soon ran into a larger stream which angled more across the ridge, instead of straight up and down. The stream ran into a larger brook, which was much wider with higher banks, and a much deeper water level. The water's noise was loud, and I proceeded to search for a natural bridge, or narrowing in which to cross. I still had a considerable distance to go crossing a large growth plot of man-planted pines and cedars. A century past, loggers had clear cut the trees and I noted some attempts by settlers to live there. Remnants of the stone foundations of their homes were still there. But they had long disappeared and Mother Earth had recaptured the land. As I walked I noted the wild apple and plum trees growing. The pine plots or groves were of different stages of size and growth, probably planted in recent times by State Park conservationists.

As I started into this region the landscape changed from the large hardwoods and hemlocks to marshy long grass and small close thick brush. Just then I caught the scent, and I decided an old buck was close by. My senses were awakened with anticipation and excitement. My experienced nose told me the smell was too strong and stinky for an old deer. It might be a big Black Bear! Now my whole body and senses were on full alert. I didn't like this type of country as it was beautiful ambush country for a bear. Many a story has been told where the hunter had been turned into the hunted by a crafty old Black Bear. Although my adrenalin and excitement were running high, I tried to keep my senses under control and calm down. I back-tracked and looked behind me frequently to confuse any bear that might be concealed in the thick bushy terrain. It was not long when the smell disappeared and my chemistry eased back to normal condition. I then followed a creek which made a large horseshoe turn leading me back behind the area in which I had been earlier.

I started chuckling to myself, thinking likely I had picked up my own scent. I decided I had better take a shower when I returned to the cabin, because that wild smell was all about me. It was no wonder earlier in the morning the young waitress had served me so quickly in a restaurant.

I proceeded on my way, feeling more at ease with myself, yet still cautious as I still had to cross the grove of pines ahead. Suddenly, before me lay strange looking animal tracks. They were round and small, yet larger than my fist. My first thought was that they were bear tracks, but as I followed them along the creek, I soon realized they were some kind of cat, most likely a lynx or bobcat.

Bear tracks are round with the cushion on the paw and the claws are on the outside and appear individually distinct. These specific tracks were round with claws on the inside of the paw imprint. These tracks were large! They indicated a very large lynx or bobcat. I didn't even think about a cougar or Mountain Lion (as they are also called).

The strange tracks wandered off away from the creek. Soon I was concentrating on any obstacles that appeared between my position and the truck. I came upon a large beaver dam. Deciding not to break a trail through there I cut across the brushy area. I made my way through and into a clearing. Suddenly, not more than twenty feet away and about twelve feet up in the air, sprawled a very large cat! He was perched in an old plum tree showing his rich dark tan winter coat. A Mountain Lion!

As the big cat glared at me I imagined, he was licking his lips relishing his next meal. Here we were, for only a few brief moments, facing each other closely. Many thoughts crossed my mind. I considered blasting the Cat out of the tree. My twelve-gauge shotgun was armed with deer slugs. The slugs are powerful enough to knock down an elephant! But, what would I do with a dead cat? Stuff it? Tan the hide? Put it in my office and keep unwanted staff out? I even thought about the endangered species I was facing. I was in a very tight, sticky situation, which required very quick and careful resolve. Somehow, I mused, I had found myself in this awkward situation often in my life. I guess I have conditioned myself to lighten up the situation with natural humour, which comes forward to ease the gravity of a situation. In this particular instance the old Laurel and Hardy comedy line came to mind. "This is a fine mess you got me into this time Ollie". I was not afraid. Instead, I put on one of my meanest looks. My eyebrows stood up and I sternly snarled. When our eyes met the cat did not see or sense any fear, and I determined from his eyes he was not sure who was going to have who for dinner. While the many thoughts flashed through my head I automatically started backstepping, putting more distance between us and allowing the cat more room. He rose, turned his head from me, sprang from the tree and dashed out of sight instantly.

In my twenty-five years of hunting in this area, I had always been skeptical of a Mountain Lion living here. Although at night I had heard their witching screams, while asking hillbilly neighbors about them. Other hunters had claimed to have caught only fleeting glimpses of them, but I remained always doubtful. I would have felt fortunate to get only a quick glimpse, let alone such a close encounter. After all these years - to experience this thrill of the wild.

It reinforces one of the poems named "Call of the Wild".

It works in me like madness, Dear
It bids me to say goodbye
For the wolf calls
The wind in the trees call,
And the full moon in the sky!

BEING FOREVER

At the rim of sunset waters
far across this great island
where mountains slant
into salt ocean
at world's end,

on a hillside there
among giant redwoods,
coyote cries the moon,
on a hillside there
where breezes scent air
with sage and cedar
and red tail hawk rides
currents of cool air,

alone there in waiting
a roundhouse of cedar
merges hill and forest,
and softly in silence
large snowflakes fall.

And snow flies here
at morning's sun
and trees their boughs
bend heavy in sleep
close by the longhouse.

It is corn hung on rafters
to dry, or storage baskets
full of acorn and pinenuts.
It is squash and beans
or smoked salmon and eel,
juniper smoke curling
from abode village
          high atop a mesa.

It is the hunter poised
at breathing hole of seal
and dugout gliding
          a maze of swamp.

There is the soft murmur
of people waiting
and dancers preparing
selves in sacred manner,
as singers hold drums
to licking flames
          and voices
begin the first cycle of
many given our people.

CANCER THE CLOAK OF DEATH

Cancer
the cloak of death
chooses victims randomly
kills almost all that gets in its path
they suffer
suffer pain once unknown
in five minutes
it kills more than
Al Capone could in a month
It's like a flame that burns eternal
try to stamp it out
and it burns you as well
like a cloak
used to smother the life within
Cancer
the great cloak of death

(dedicated to Bill Ice - in memory)

DOG ROAD WOMAN

They called you
grandma
Maggie like
Maggie Valley
I called on you
for your knowledge
of pieced cotton
I worked clay
to pottery
and thread to weave
but had no frame
nor understanding
of pattern
in quilting.
Climbing high
in sacred wood,
which feeds the
di ni la wi gi u no do ti,
I captured hickory
twigs you wanted
for a toothbrush
to dip snuff.
Ninety-two year old
leathered fingers
caressed stitch

and broadcloth
into blanket.
You with your apron
and bonnet
and laughter
at gold dollars
and processed meats.
You who taught
me to butcher
without waste
and who spun
stories on your
card whenever I
would listen,
we fashioned stars.

Jane Inyallie

WEBS

The automated spider
of today spins
miles of complex
luminescent fibres.
Held by gigantic
metal poles in
concrete jungles.

Through woven
microbiotic fibre
we hear rapid
fragmented muted
voices, linked to
a network of broken
patterns of speech.

Caught in
the web of
sterile
impersonal
corporate
technology.

In spider's
massive
memory banks
neatly filed
away are
long forgotten
ways of how
a spider spins
a simple web.

GETTING IN

Whispy white hair
Draped over her naked
Body.

Flanks and breasts sagging,
Hanging.

Hints of stretchmarks.
Childbirth.
Bellyflap conceals,
Hides grey pubic
Hair.

Toenails, thick, rigid, almost
Grey.

Tatooed on her hand,
Raven.

Recollections of childhood,
Puberty.

Charcoaled forever.

Loose skinfolds from arms.
Held babies living and
Dead.

Loving embraces with their father.

Louise Profeit-LeBlanc

She dips a toe in the water.
Slowly, carefully. Shaking,
Lowers in stiff legs and
Torso.

Releasing a long sigh. Denoting
Fond appreciation of life's still
Lasting pleasures.

The Bath!

CASTLES AND MISSILES

Castle towers starkly silhouetting
        against the sky
        high and mighty
        even with gaping holes
                in their walls
        still they thrust upward
        monumenting
        over the land
        of plain folk.

Ruins now many
        such castles
        strike one as harmless
        like an old crag of stone
        haunted perhaps
        by evil deeds
        and torture chambers
        but visitors
        now may come
        and go.

Perhaps it is
        that some white people
        have been disappointed
        that we had no castles
        in America,
        America of the Indians,
        no stone fortresses
        withering away
        under sun and rain.

The meaning though
I will inform
lest you be deceived,
there is a vast difference
between America of the Indians
and Europe,
they were <u>not</u> the same.

We had,
the southwestern pueblos
our vast apartment houses
our temple-mounds, Cahokia,
our fortified villages
our effigy earth-works--
but castles
we had none.

Castles,
were not simply buildings
nor were they villages
but forts
strongholds
rising high
with armoured might
above the people.

The castles speak,
telling of tyranny,
they tell us of greed,
they speak of a world
we have come to know
too well
in these latter days.

Castles moan
of the destruction of the European tribes
of the doing away with
democratic communities
of the disappearance of the
free and open country
of the birth of robber barons
and rich men, of feudalism
and power.

Castles whisper to us
of control
of dominance
of lords
peering from towers
over rolling lands
below
peopled by the descendants
of those who once were
owners of it all.

Once, it is said,
there were no earls, dukes,
and counts,
no lords behind walls
to collect tribute, taxes,
rents, swordsmen and judges
in one.

But the people were conquered
conquered by a breed
of knights, of fighters
who
generation after generation
schemed and plotted
to make greater and greater
their power and wealth.

Murderers, they killed,
fornicators, they made sons,
rapists, they seized women,
opportunists, they gathered up
widows
with estates, of course,
and castles,
always castles.

Castles of wood and thatch, then
castles of stone,
castles with a tower, then
castles with many towers,
growing larger
and larger
against each other,
against the people.

Schemers, the bloody-handed
the barons
now with the king
now with a challenger
now for Scotland
now for England
no matter
for winning is what counted,
not loyalty to a nation.

Sir Andrew Leslie of Aberdeenshire
it is recorded
had seventy children
he lost eleven sons at Harlaw
lost thirteen at Banochy
fornicated with seven women
at different houses
in one night
had seven women pregnant at one time
carried off by force
the Maid of Strathdon
producing a son by her
while his patient wife gave gifts
to all of his bastards
what else could she do?

And Alexander Stewart, the Wolf of Badenoch,
brother to a king,
seized a wife to get her estate
got her title
and reigned supreme
raiding churches
condemned but never punished
(who could punish him?)

It was
scheme carefully
greedy baron
see who has the power
who has the available daughter
who has the right to
grant
the land
and the people
to you.

And so the castles tell us
walls of stone
to protect the wicked
from the people
walls of stone
to protect the treasures
stolen
here and there
walls of stone
to hide the tortures
of any who dared
to dissent

But more they tell us,
of greedy men
protected,
of a culture of differences
of classes
of rich and poor
of the
enshrinement
of patriarchy
of aggression.

And this, we know,
is why
when the British
and the Spanish
and the others
came to America
they acted the way they did.

This, my friends,
is why the restless,
aggressive temperament
is still with us
the materialism
and the endless search
for wealth.

Today, we no longer
castles fear
in their place
we find
headquarters for police
and army bases
bombs and missiles,
for a new race of barons
have new tactics--
same old strategy.

The people used the cannons
the castles to destroy
but they did not destroy
the culture of greed
and before they could
the barons seized
the cannons
and turned them
against the people.

Jack Forbes

No, we never had castles
in America
before the Europeans came
but now
we have the towers of missiles,
of the Pentagon
and Standard Oil
and Bechtel
and isn't it all the same?

The way of the castles
of the robber barons
of the aristocracy of
avarice
has been carried
to the four corners
of the world.

And, yes,
the destruction of free
tribal peoples,
small communities,
still goes on
and we curse in the dark
and vote for another car
and a new color TV.

CHANGED IT:
Revolutionary Methodology/
Indian Voodoo Technology

Walking it backwards
tricking it loose
words about sideways
cooked somebodies goose

free as an arrow
twisting in fame
thought bending it somehow
would recycle shame

looking back two ways
and shrugging off price
the politics of bad math
is the square root of strife

Kimberly Blaeser

ICE TRICKSTERS AND SHADOW STORIES FOR JERRY

I.

Later that winter she began to hear voices.
No insistent whispers of conscience,
Not the teasing of her muse,
Voices of ice, ice voices,
Tinkling like wind chimes,
        the coated branches of trees,
Waking her again at night,
        banging and booming across the wide expanse of
        frozen lake,
Ice, a delicate porcelain,
        shattering with a hollow pop beneath her feet;
Screeching beneath the sled runners,
mock pain echoing in winter silence.

II.

Her companions all deaf to the diamond poetry of ice
She, fearing the beauty, the coming of this new ice age,
Listened in trembling search to sounds become voices
Become words become shadow stories of ice.
Recalling the mystery of ice point,
        the temperature of equilibrium of pure water
        and ice;
Remembering the story, how ice woman froze the windigoo
        at just that point in the moccasin game.
Having sought herself that delicate equilibrium
                between recklessness and cowering,
Knowing truly how the balance of story sustains two natures,
                she began to imagine, ice shadows.

For Africa's ice plant, a trickster story:
        fleshy leaves covered with glistening crystals,
A suspended transformation, a metaphor for life,
        like the evil gambler frozen by ancient ice woman,
Like delicate ice needles, floating in midair,
        finding the circumstances to defy gravity.
Suspended herself, frozen in winter time, an ice floe
        looked happily in a glacial epoch,
trickling, tinkling, cracking, booming
Ice tricksters telling a story
She began to hear.

III.

Hearing, too, at last,
        their sounding the metaphors of death,
In the trees, limbs enveloped in glitter,
On the ledge, spikes honed of crystal water,
Both incandescent, resplendent with their sun death
Ice capsules weeping their own doom, icicles crashing to earth.
Angry now, she skated madly by the moon's light,
Feigning indifference, ignoring the screaming sound
When her blades cut a fresh path across the hardened lake,
Believing somehow she was forestalling breakup, melt-down, spring.
Knowing human things like refrigeration and dry ice,
Believing in the science of Celsius and centigrade,
Thinking ice trickster to be of water and winter,
Subject to simple laws of time and temperature,
Forgetting temporarily the ice shadows cast by myth.

IV.

Then falling one night asleep or beneath the ice,
Finding herself pulled from dream or watery death,
To waken damp with memories of a silent ice woman.
Wondering had she been rescued or been condemned,
Wondering if she was human, or ice, or shadow,
Wondering if her voice sounded or was silent,
Wondering if her story was the present or the past,
Wondering if she was a myth or reality,
Wondering finally, if perhaps they weren't the same,
At least the same, in that mysterious center,
        that ice point of consciousness,
        that place of timeless equilibrium
        where one begins at last to understand voices.

THANKS

Thanks for today and tomorrow
Thanks for yesterday and the day before
Thanks for what you have taught us
Thanks for everything and even more
Thanks for the gift of laughter
Thanks for the gift of song
Thanks for seeing our point of view
For the road may be hard and long.

HIS CASTLE

He built a castle
on a mountain
so high above the lies
the iron towers rise.
A screaming sun is born
when he unlocks the doors
locked by his father's roars,
his heart searches
for the beat of the clock
hiding within the
mountain rock.
"Reveal your relative sin"
I asked him
and his eyes got dim...
he raged and howled with
his look scowled.
On the mountain he is king
and with his dark eyes
he sings a song
laced with lyrics of ire
that forever stir and sting.
On the walls he raised
he paints self portrait
everyday in a new way.
He sits on his throne
with his paint brush in constant evolution
creating a forgiving solution:
MOTHER AND FATHER
STAND HAND IN HAND
"Will you come and walk with me?"
he asked me kindly.
I took his small hand
and we walked through his land.

UNTITLED

I saw the little big man
gripping life with all eight of his fingers.
He hid high on ceilings and pulled close into
corners. He moved smooth and silent
and built webs as delicate as life.

Mary Lawrence

THE CHIPPEWA WOMAN

The frail old Chippewa woman
ripened with age
combs her
frosted strands
of long,
lustrous thin hair

With pale yellow
deep sunken eyes
deeply moulded
each crack and crease
lines of primitive and distinct
haunted, lonely face.

On rickety wooden floor
unvarnished and slivered
stinking damp of decay
in remote distant village
she sits and rocks
in wobbly, worn antique rocking chair
rested are thin bony feet,
dangled over hand-made worn out stool.
Scratching with long feeble fingers
she coils and squirms
wrenched body
slowly she shifts
and gazes placidly.

Valiantly,
straight ahead
closely she watches
the Grandfather clock
slowly tick
one chime!
two chimes!
three chimes!
Effortlessly...
she blinks her tired eyes
and drifts
far away to distant shores
of youthful play
to the blue-grass hills
spawning river banks
sitting beneath the warm shade
of the weeping willow trees
She watches
by the hour
bright red female salmon
fighting to swim upstream
through swift currents, until
rest finally comes,
their spawned ground.

She smiles
in soothing pleasant memory.
The drift of pinewood
tingles her nostrils
she savours
its pleasant earthy scent.

Mary Lawrence

She scowls
awakened in muse
and wraps her shawl
tightly around
soft worn shoulders.
Warmed are
her battered bones
worn and torn
over rugged years.

She turns in her rocking chair
and stares
with wide-open hollow eyes,
again she recalls
Hardship Falls
nestled in the foothills
of Mount Steepville
and all the little fish
unscathed, unbarred.

She remembers
her closest kin
half-hearted Aunt Ruth, miserly Uncle Ned
Brother Bart, Innocent sister Anne,
Some long gone
Some still alive.

In her afternoon drift
the thing she longed
Most
Seemed hardest
Yet...

Her eyes closed
Her mind departed
she pulled her shawl tightly
around her ghostly frame
and breathed
her last few gasps
of the past
of the present...
Peacefully
she welcomed
her spawning ground.

SIT DOWN

Eat this feast I have
prepared for you,
Drink the water I pour for you
and a gentle rain shall kiss
your craving.
Give yourself freedom
with your smile...
laugh and be beautiful
as you gently beguile.

ANCESTOR POEM

Last night the bear was my ancestor
Last night the bear was my memory
trembling at the rustle outside my door

Last night the bear was my ancestor
Last night the bear was my memory
moving through the bushes
frightening me into stone

Last night the bear was my ancestor
Last night the bear was my memory
circling the high rock I stood on
sure there was no safe place

Last night the bear was my ancestor
Last night the bear was my memory
circling through underbush unseen
breeding remembrance into my body
with every ripple
crushing the underbush at his feet

Last night the bear was my ancestor
Last night the bear was my memory
returning to heal me
this bear is returning to heal me

Al Hunter

Last night the bear was my ancestor
Last night the bear was my memory
speaking with the tenderness of old men

When I hear your voices
calling from four directions
they filled my ears like prayers
Your voices pulled me from my slumber
The pungent sage pulled me near to you

When I came from the north
I saw you praying
your body wrapped in smoke
It was you who called me
to that place on rock
to read the prayers in your body
as it quaked from the fear of me

I saw your feathers shaking
I saw your altar on stone
I saw a shadow like wisps of memory
I saw the years in between

I entered your pipe
when you drew the last breath of it
I filled your body with healing
and did not bruise you.

CULTURAL DECOLONIZATION

What is the nature of cultural decolonization? It is a new focus on the understanding and awareness of Indian/Métis culture and history from an authentic aboriginal perspective and sensitivity. It is a readjustment of white mainstream culture and history which has served as justification for conquest and continued imperial domination. Moreover it is a reverse interpretation. It shows that conquest and occupation by European imperialists was a step backwards in the evolution of aboriginal civilization. If our country had not been invaded by European mercenaries 500 years ago, our indigenous civilization would have been much further advanced and more fully developed in all dimensions: economically, politically, culturally, ecologically, and particularly in civilized humanity. The work of decolonizing our culture and history is a monumental task. It wipes from our people's consciousness the sense of colonization and inferiorization. In doing so, we put before our people an image of a historically well organized socio-economic system and a developed civilization. We learn how our ancestors were conquered and how the culture was devastated. Aboriginal civilization has a past that is worth studying. It was a dynamic society, evolving and progressive; not static and archaic. This is one of the greatest white supremacy myths that must be rejected, and made truthful.

Cultural decolonization means perceiving knowledge in terms of a specific place and time as a principle of intellectual inquiry. For Métis, Indians and Inuit the place is Canada, and the time is imperial capitalism. The place provides a perimeter for historical and cultural analysis. It allows our historians and authors to use a critical analysis of British and French colonialism. One of the first tasks of cultural decolonization is to analyze and interpret our history and culture from an aboriginal perspective. This is one of the important steps in our re-awakening. It is the key to transforming the colonizer's society that continues to dominate us.

Aboriginal centric history - the interpretation of Indian/Métis history from an aboriginal perspective has no European heroes. There are only Indian/Métis warriors and the supportive masses. Beginning with the brilliant Iroquois resistance wars which ended in driving out the French mercenaries from Indian territory, to the heroic wars of Pontiac and his warriors who defeated the British, to the liberation wars of the Métis at Red River and Batoche, and finally to the history of our liberation struggles in the 1960's and 70's. The national liberation movement of the 1960's was the first militant re-awakening since 1885 at Batoche, and one of the most outstanding people's struggle in terms of confronting the colonizer and promoting counter-consciousness among our people.

Who will write the aboriginal centric history and culture? Those Métis, Indian and Inuit persons with an authentic aboriginal consciousness and sense of nationhood. That is, persons who have been born in and grown up in a reserve or Métis community. Without an indigenous consciousness it is not possible to write true indigenous centric history or literature. They must hold a counter-consciousness, as well as social values, attitude and ethic that are integral to the Indian/Métis colonies. Their goals and future must be seen within or associated with our people and communities. Collaborator leaders and associates, government funded elites and main-stream opportunists cannot contribute to aboriginal culture and history. They are only tourists and exploiters in our homeland.

Those of us who have lived in colonized micro-societies have been subjected to the suppressive weight of dehumanization and non-intellectual thought imposed by the colonizer. As a result we hold feelings of discontent and challenge; having sensed the obliteration of intellectual activity and the forced 'backwardness' in our community. How deeply I felt the eurocentric repression against our Métis culture and history. I lived only fifteen miles from the glory of our ancestors' heroic struggles at Batoche, but that `glory' rung in our ears as a hideous defeat. Anglo superiority stigmatized and smeared us into muteness. At the sound of the last gun, eurocentric historians rushed in to write and publish their distorted myths that flooded the nation. These white supremacy scribes swelled the flow of aboriginal blood and forced our people into shameful hiding from the odium of their weird and distorted descriptions. Such academic myths are typically used to subjugate the oppressed into deeper colonization and ghettoization. Myths and falsehoods not only structured Métis and Indian culture and history, but at the same time justified brutal military rule. As historians and authors we must repudiate these fabrications and write a genuine account of our ancestors' struggles and victories.

Decolonization and liberation cannot take place without counter-consciousness and a spirit of devotion to the cause of self-determination, justice and equality. There are some excellent aboriginal centric historical and cultural works emerging from our brilliant Indian/ Métis/Inuit scholars, authors and poets. The greatest break-through in the analysis and interpretation in aboriginal centric history is the work of Ron Bourgeault. In his ground-breaking theories and writings he explores the intentional devastating changes of traditional communal society to European mercantilists for the purpose of exploitation and control. Bourgeault presents a new perspective in aboriginal centric history, as well as providing a new theoretical basis for emerging aboriginal intellectuals. Several other outstanding aboriginal creations from a centric perspective have been produced by Maria Campbell, Jeannette Armstrong, Lee Maracle, Emma Laroque, Duke Redbird and others. Aboriginal centricity is a study of the masses 'from below' with a view to the inarticulate and poorly educated people. Therefore, our style of writing must be uncomplicated; a popular, journalists style, and not the academic or esoteric type.

The important factor about these people and their creations is the perspective. They make a clear break from the Euro-Canadian white supremacy interpretation, the typical racists, sterotyped image of Indian-Métis-Inuit (IMI) to a new factual aboriginal perspective. They are working from their critical counter-consciousness. Their works could not have been produced without it. Also, they live in close relationships and experiences with IMI communities, which are vital for the aboriginal creations. In this renaissance period, we must write with and as part of the IMI people; not for them. Explanations to the white mainstream population is not our major concern. Writing and speaking to members of a quasi-apartheid society does not change their attitudes or ideology . That can be done only by changing the structure and institutions of the state. Establishment white historians argue that Indians and Métis have no past worthy of study. To them, we are an illiterate, primitive mass who have no sense of 'peoplehood'. But, as aboriginal people, we know differently. We must not only challenge, but must transcend these distorted falsehoods that have stood for so long as legitimate history.

The most ruthless tactic employed by the neocolonial state was to inflict on our people Indian/Métis collaborators, leaders and organizations with powerful generous grants of money that fractured our liberation struggle and crushed our spirited momentum in the 1970's from which it has not yet recovered. This served to abruptly halt our movement towards political emancipation and cultural revitalization. To a large extent, however, these comprador bravadoes have been marginalized and reduced to considerable irrelevance and ineffectuality. Therefore, as IMI artists and intellectuals we should take the opportunity to move forward in terms of authentic culture and history, hopefully without internal conflict. As colonized people, it is inevitable that we will have differing points of view and aims. But that is par for every colony and its peoples. We need only to call to mind the black people of South Africa, Sri Lanka and Somali, it is the imperialist's most powerful parting strategy: to divide and war among ourselves internally, hoping that the colonized will call him back. But his interests have now turned to selling armaments to both sides.

The corporate rulers have structured and perfected a neocolonial state and saddled it on our people; with new suppressive strategies that served to disperse and confuse all progressive activists. Other elites are co-opted in to the middle class mainstream society with jobs that 'go nowhere'. It is now the task of IMI intellectuals, authors, academics and activists who possess an aboriginal consciousness to analyze and understand the 'how' of our new form of oppression and powerlessness. The silence of the 1960's liberation struggle was not a defeat, but a temporary diversion. Now, we must sharpen our analytical tools for future challenges and nation building.

LeAnne Howe

HASHI MI MALI (SUN AND WIND)
FOR KEN (THREE EAGLES) BORDEAUX

I

Each Morning, *Hashi*, the stark red creator rises,
swelling,
she passes over the ground, spilling a drop or two of her blood
which grows the corn, and the people: Choctaw that is we.
Naked, she goes down on us,
her flaming hair burns us brown.
Finally, in the month of *Tek Inhashi*, the Sun of Women,
when we are navel deep in red sumac, we cut the leaves and
smoke to her success. Sing her praises.
Hashi, Creator Sun, won't forget.

II

When *Ohoyo Ikbi* pulled
freshly-made Choctaw
out of her red thighs,
we were very wet, so
one-by-one,
she stacked us
on the mound,
and *Hashi* kissed our
bodies with her morning lips
and painted our faces with afternoon fire,
and, in the month of *Hashi Hoponi*, the Sun of Cooking,
we were made

III

It is said that
once-a-month warriors can kill a thing with spit.
So when the soldiers came,
our mothers stood on the tops of the
ramparts and made the *tashka* call
urging their men on.
Whirling their tongues and hatchets in rhythm,
they pulled red water and fire from their bodies
and covered their chests with bullet-proof blood.
And when it was over,
they made a fire bed on the prairie that
blew across the people like a storm;
melded our souls with iron.
And in the month of *Hashi Mali*, the Sun of Wind,
that still urge us on
at sunrise.

RAIN

Roaring down
on cars and windows
Trying to get in.
Flooding all the roads
and dancing through the sky.
Making a swimming pool
out of my front yard.
Splashing in the puddles.

Evan Tlesla Adams

JANICE'S CHRISTMAS

(The following is a monologue written for the New Play Centre's production of "Voices of Christmas" at the Vancouver East Cultural Centre, December, 1992. It is a retelling of actual events that occurred when I was a little boy, during Christmas, 1972.)

Christmas ended for my family when I was five years old, back home on the rez. Some days before Christmas, Old Mabel's house across from the graveyard had burned down and three of my cousins had died. That same night, my sister Janice - she was eight - asked my father, "What happens when you die?" He was quiet for a moment, then he answered, "You go to heaven." "I know," she said, "you sit in the arms of Jesus."

The next day, my dad was at work and my mom was at her sister's. My eldest sister Rose was looking after us. She was fourteen. All us kids were running around the yard as we usually do on a Sunday morning. Morgan, the boy from next door, came outside. He had a rifle. He said he was going to shoot some birds. All us boys ran along behind him into the smokehouse. He closed the door behind us. Pretty soon, we heard a "knock, knock, knock." Morgan opened the door - all these little girls looking up at him. "Go away," he yelled and slammed the door, right on the tip of his rifle. Bang! Right near my face. A little girl started to scream.

Morgan opened the smokehouse door just in time to see one of the girls fall. She was crying, "My arm, my arm!" By her long hair, I could tell it was my sister Janice. Morgan ran and picked her up and started to run towards our house. We all ran along behind him. He was so fast he left us all behind. Up the stairs he went. But the door was locked. He started to kick the door. I caught up to him and I remember looking up at him as he moved. Janice's long hair swung back and forth as he turned. Finally Rose opened the door. "What did you do to her", she cried. "I shot her!" "What did you do to her?" "I shot her.: Over and over again she kept asking, not understanding. Then she began to cry hysterically.

Morgan pushed his way inside and lay Janice on the couch. Rose calmed down enough to phone our mom. "Just come home," she said. We waited. We didn't know how to call the police or how to call an ambulance.

Finally someone said, "Look for a bullet hole!" So we took off her jacket and pulled down her dress. Nothing. We looked on her coat and found a small hole in the shoulder. So we looked at her shoulder. There was a tiny mark, so small it wasn't even bleeding. By this time, Janice was unconscious. Then we heard gurgling noises in her chest. Morgan blew into her mouth, then pressed down hard on her chest. Blood poured out of her mouth like thick paint, across her face, down the side of the couch and onto the floor.

Then my mom came in. [pause] She just stood by the couch...Nothing. A woman told me once that mothers live with the thought that something might happen to their children. My mother looked, and I think she knew, she knew that Janice was dead.

A few days later, we had the wake. I'll always remember it because it was my sister Maureen's seventh birthday. The house was full of chrysanthemums and I'll always remember having to steer around this white coffin, sitting in the middle of everything. I started to cry that night - not because I was sad, but because I was scared, scared of Janice's ghost. My father wouldn't even look at me as I cried, he was so disgusted with me. But my mother picked me up, carried me into her bedroom and lay with me until I fell asleep, even though the house was full of people.

The next day, after the mass, the coffin was opened up and everybody lined up to see the body one last time. I remember someone lifting me up so I could look at her. Janice had been an extraordinarily pretty little girl; not the little, tiny beauty of little white girls, but the broad, healthy look of an eight-year old native girl. But now she looked grey and blank, her long hair pulled so you couldn't see it.

At the graveyard, my mother fell. Suddenly she just went, "Ohhh!" and she fell. I think if sisters hadn't been there, she might have fallen into the grave.

Just before Christmas, I had to go to court to testify. I was so small, I didn't even fit on the witness stand. So the judge stood me on his desk and held onto my feet. He told everyone, "This is a very smart boy and I want you to tell everyone here what happened that day." So I did, and as I was telling them, I looked down. There, scattered across the judge's desk, were pictures of Janice, naked, lying on a table - photographs from her autopsy that he had left out.

The coroner later explained that the bullet had passed through both her lungs and tipped her heart, she didn't have a chance. He ruled her death accidental.

A few days later, it was Christmas. Everyone was trying to be bright and happy for a change. I was so excited. Even my mom had a nice little smile on. We all sat around the tree, opening our presents. We open our presents in order. I was the last one. I was so excited - my present was big and square and HEAVY. Finally, it was my turn! I tore it open, and inside was a great, big...dictionary. [pause] I started to cry. I didn't want to...My father was so disgusted with me, he wouldn't even look at me. But my mother leaned in close and said, "Evan, you're a smart boy. You can get out of this place."

It's been twenty years since that Christmas, and my family hasn't talked about it one bit. But maybe this year, we will. Maybe we'll have a little memorial ceremony for Janice out in the yard, like we should have done. Maybe we'll get to remember her brief life instead of her horrible death. But I have to ask, what does a child's death at Christmas mean? And I'll finally get to ask my sisters, and my mother and my father, "Do you really think she's sitting in the arms of Jesus?"

[Author's note: the telling of this story was not to make the audience aware of my personal tragedy as a First Nations person. Rather it is told as an affirmation to all those people - especially other First Nations people - who carry loss and tragedy into the celebration of events like Jesus' birth - a man, in whose name, many of have been persecuted, punished, stolen - even murdered.

SEE THIS PEN?

The pen is a blade
the paper flesh
it rips
tears
slices
to bleed the answers
between the spine

The pen is sharpened
on whetstone logic
it must know that the Alternating Current will throw
a million spiders up your arm
it must know that the Direct Current will burn you
five inches deep and three inches through

The pen must rehearse with whispering lips
the pauses
the punches
the silence of the piece

The pen is a soldier
folding blades in the black
knowing anatomy
and the ways to cripple
knowing anatomy
and the ways to heal

When others turn away from the horror
the pen must move closer
must stick its tongue in the corpse's mouth
to taste that last mint
to breathe that last smoke

When someone's arching their back in a grunting pump
the pen must hop on
help push
must cry out with them
must collapse
must record who came
who went
who stayed behind
and who fell screaming
The pen was born with its eyes sewn open
the pen a blade
the paper flesh

William George

A JOURNEY TO EXPRESSION

On Turtle Island there is a path. On Turtle Island there are many paths. On one path stood a shell, a giant clam shell. In the shell a lonely human struggled. He banged on the shell. He thrust himself about in his confinement wishing it would vanish. Knees, legs, arms, and back cramped under stress. He was suffocating. He gasped for air. Muggy, stale vapours enveloped the dark. A scream, his scream penetrated the shell. A scream unheard. A scream unanswered.

A person walked down this path. The Walker walked around the shell.

"I thought I heard something. No, it was nothing."

The walker did not hear the scream. The scream that was stifled for over five hundred years. The scream that never was to escape the lips of many generations. The walker did not hear the screamer, a new screamer. He was The Silent Screamer. The Silent Screamer was a human trapped in a clam shell. His flesh and spirit were entangled in the closing.

A man and woman walked down this path. Beckon and Hope stopped. Beckon held out his hand.

"Listen, do you hear that sound? It is very faint."

"Yes, I hear it. Someone is in there."

"Hello in there. Beckon and Hope are here."

"Hey! I climbed in this shell! I can't get out! Can you help me?"

"We can barely hear you. We will try to open the shell."

Beckon and Hope reached their hands into the mouth of the shell in an attempt to pry it open. Beckon and Hope did all they could to help. All of their effort did not release The Silent Screamer.

"It is impossible to open the shell from the outside. You have to open it yourself," Beckon stated.

"Close your eyes and accept where you are. Totally embrace who you are," Hope instructed.

The Silent Screamer stopped banging. He stopped screaming. He stopped fighting. The Silent Screamer closed his eyes. He began accepting where he was. He accepted.

"Yes, something is happening. Something is changing."

The giant clam shell transformed into an egg shell. A shell preparing for birth, preparing for re-birth. One small crack pierced through the resistance. The Silent Screamer slowly emerged out of the shell.

"Brother, you made it."

The giant egg shell shattered and vanished. The Silent Screamer breathed. He put out his hand to shake with Beckon and Hope.

"Hello, my name is Beckon."

"Hello, I am Hope."

"Hello, I am Screamer Freed. Thank you for your help. I screamed till my lungs nearly burst. No one heard. No one stopped."

"It is okay now you are out," Hope assured him.

"That shell is so impenetrable from the outside. Sometimes it takes a scream to voice a whisper," Beckon said.

"Yes, that is true. Sometimes it only takes a whisper. A whisper and someone to listen," Hope stated.

The three stood on the path.

"Now where do I go?" asked the Screamer Freed.

"That is your choice."

"Close your eyes again and listen," Hope instructed.

The Screamer Freed closed his eyes. He heard some buzz. He heard muffled murmurs. He concentrated and listened.

"Path, walk your path."

The Screamer Freed heard the cedar. He heard the blades of grass. He heard the trickle of a stream.

"I will walk. The answer was within me. Deep in my gut the answer was there, I just had to listen. All around me and all within me I hear those whispers you've been talking about."

"Okay, remember to listen to those guiding whispers and voice those whispers," Beckon said.

"Thank-you, Beckon and Hope, for helping me help myself. Farewell, my brother and sister."

"Good-bye, brother, take care."

Beckon and Hope left The Screamer Freed to walk his path. He walked and sang in accompaniment with the songs in the wind. The Screamer Freed danced down his path. It was in that moment when music was more than music, song was more than song, dance was more than dance. For him everything started to look like bits and pieces of a whole. The Screamer Freed continued his journey with a different perspective. It was a feeling. He felt a connectedness with the world around him.

"I believe I was born with this feeling. I'm so grateful to have an opportunity to experience this feeling again. A feeling I now know I pushed away."

One step at a time. One foot in front of the other; he made his way down the path. The Screamer Freed stopped walking when he came to a giant shell; someone else's shell was lying in the middle of the path. He bent down towards the shell and lightly tapped on it.

"Hello, is someone in there?"

"No! Go away! Everything is fine! Just fine I tell you!"

"Hey, I understand. I was in my own shell just recently. I know what it's like. Wanna talk about it?"

"No! There's nothing to talk about! I am fine I tell you! Go away! Leave me alone!"

The Screamer Freed had to realize that this screamer wanted to stay where he was. That was his choice.

"Choices, that's it. We all have choices to make. I make my choices and let others make their own choices."

The Screamer Freed began to walk his path. He was having second thoughts about leaving his shell.

"Maybe I should have stayed. It could have been safer. Maybe it wasn't so bad a place to be."

Eagle's piercing shrill echoed in the sky. The Screamer Freed watched with respect as Eagle soared. Eagle spread his wings and flew over the meadow, flew over the path. He scanned the contours of the bumpy path that lay in front of the Screamer Freed. Eagle descended from sky to earth. Eagle swooped down and again ascended into the sky. The Screamer Freed raised his arms to Eagle, raised his arms to sky.

"I made the right choice for me. I will walk."

Eagle soared into the horizon. The Screamer Freed walked his path on his journey to expression.

A MARRIAGE OF CONVEYANCE

WOG, carrying POG, enters and comes to a stop.

WOG: Excuse me, Pog. I don't like to bother you.
POG: Well. What is it then?
WOG: I hope this won't put you out.
POG: Thank you, Wog. I hope not to be put out.
WOG: Pog, I'm tired.
POG: Pardon me.
WOG: I'm tired.
POG: No, Wog, you're not tired.
WOG: I'm not?
POG: No, you're not.
WOG: Oh. But I feel tired.
POG: You don't look tired. At all. You don't feel tired. You feel strong.
WOG: Excuse me, Pog. I do feel tired.
POG: And you don't smell tired. You smell strong.
WOG: Oh don't! That tickles.
POG: And you don't even taste tired. At all. You taste quite fresh.
WOG: I do?
POG: You do. Quite fresh. Quite strong. You can't possibly be tired. At all.
WOG: You're sure, Pog?
POG: I'm quite certain, Wog. It only goes to show.
WOG: Oh. (walks a few steps and stops again) Excuse me, Pog, I don't like to bother you. I do feel tired.
POG: You do.

WOG:	I do.
POG:	Well. What are we going to do?
WOG:	Rest?
POG:	Rest?
WOG:	Yes.
POG:	You know, you're right.
WOG:	I know I'm right.
POG:	Stand still then.
WOG:	All right. (pause) Pog, excuse me, please.
POG:	Have you finished standing still?
WOG:	No. I just had a thought.
POG:	That's not good for you, you know.
WOG:	I know.
POG:	Standing still is good, you know.
WOG:	I know. (pause) Now Pog, I'll just set you down--
POG:	What? Wog, stop. Stop it! Stop it, please!
WOG:	Just for a moment, Pog.
POG:	Stop it stop it stop it stop it!
WOG:	All right all right. (pause) All right, Pog.
POG:	Quite all right, Wog.
WOG:	Pog, please. Let me set you down.
POG:	No.
WOG:	Please?
POG:	Don't ask.
WOG:	Why? Why, Pog?
POG:	Pardon me, Wog, but did you forget again?
WOG:	Forget?
POG:	You forgot.
WOG:	Did I?
POG:	You forgot that it isn't right.
WOG:	It isn't right?
POG:	It's wrong. Pardon me, Wog, but we promised. Remember? Wog?
WOG:	Yes. We did promise.

POG: What did we promise?
WOG: I don't know.
POG: What did we promise?
WOG: I had a thought. But it's hard to hold.
POG: Tell me, Wog.
WOG: Excuse me, Pog, please let me set you down first.
POG: Wog, stop! Oh help! Help! Help help!
WOG: Who're you calling?
POG: Help.
WOG: But I'm here.
POG: Oh Wog. (pause) You know the answer.
WOG: I guess I do.
POG: What did we promise?
WOG: You tell me. Please.
POG: You shouldn't frown so hard.
WOG: I know. Oh I know.
POG: Well?
WOG: We promised, we promised to love, honour and, and convey?
POG: And don't I love you? Don't I? And don't I honour you? Wog?
WOG: I guess so.
POG: Wog!
WOG: I mean yes, you do.
POG: Well?
WOG: It is the least I can do to carry you.
POG: You know, you're right.
WOG: Yes, I know. (pause) But, couldn't I just set you down?
POG: Wog, you know I can't bear to be separate from you. You know that?
WOG: Separate?
POG: Yes.
WOG: That's the love part.

POG: You know, you're right.
WOG: Yes. (pause) But couldn't I just stand you here?
POG: What?
WOG: I'll keep my arms around you.
POG: Oh Wog! How can you be so nasty?
WOG: Oh I'm sorry. (pause) Pog. How am I mean to you?
POG: You know I can't stand. You know my legs are no good.
WOG: I guess I forgot. I'm sorry.
POG: You know how I'm broken.
WOG: Yes, I do.
POG: You remembered all along.
WOG: No. I forgot.
POG: You know how I got broken.
WOG: I know, Pog.
POG: I'd stand. You know that. I'd do anything if I could. But I'm broken.
WOG: I know.
POG: You want to throw me away.
WOG: No, Pog, I don't.
POG: Who broke me? Who?
WOG: I'm sorry, Pog.
POG: I'm broken. I'm useless. That's what you think.
WOG: No I don't.
POG: I'm just a thing to play with. Pardon me, Wog, but you throw broken toys away, don't you?
WOG: Yes, I guess so.
POG: Go on. Put me down.
WOG: Please, Pog, I don't like this.
POG: I'll get a bad cold. I'll freeze. You'll be better alone.

WOG: Alone?
POG: You'll be able to run.
WOG: Run?
POG: Run. To go fast. Like we did before.
WOG: Like before. Fast.
POG: Like flying.
WOG: Flying?
POG: Yes. Like having wings.
WOG: Flying. Yes. Flying. Flying!
POG: Yes.
WOG: Do you see me flying?
POG: No. You know I don't.
WOG: I do?
POG: You know you threw me away. I'm dead.
WOG: Don't say that stuff.
POG: I'm broken. Broken and useless--Ouch! Don't pinch.
WOG: Don't say that. I picked you up.
POG: Put me down.
WOG: I caught you.
POG: You'll be better alone.
WOG: No. You're not broken. Not useless. At all.
POG: But it hurts.
WOG: There. There. Kisses make it better?
POG: Kisses make it better. I guess.
WOG: You're not useless. Pog, you remind me.
POG: I do?
WOG: When I forget.
POG: Sometimes it's good to forget bad stuff.
WOG: It's good to remember, too.
POG: Pardon me, Wog, but is that true?
WOG: I like to carry you. It's the honour part.
POG: You know, you're right.
WOG: And you make me strong.
POG: I do?

WOG: Yes. And you kiss me.
POG: Pardon me, Wog. You don't want to put me down.
WOG: No, Pog. I'm not tired. At all.
POG: Well, that's it then.

WOG, carrying POG, walks off.

THE END

Author Biographies

(Please note that biographical information was not available from all contributing authors.)

Evan Tlesla Adams is a twenty-six year old Coast Salish from the Sliammon Band near Powell River, B.C. Evan is an alumnus of St. Michael's University School and of Lester B. Pearson College of the Pacific, both of Victoria. In 1988, his original play "Dreams of Sleep" was selected as one of Canada's entries to the International Festival of Young Playwrights in Sydney, Australia. He wrote the award-winning audio tour of the First Peoples Gallery at the Royal British Columbia Museum in Victoria. Another of his plays, Snapshots, has been presented in more than 300 communities.

Jeannette Armstrong is a writer and the Director of the School of Writing at the En'owkin Centre in Penticton, British Coumbia. Previously published in BORDER CROSSINGS, 1992

Maxine Rose Baptiste is an Okanagan from the Osoyoos Reserve in B.C. She is currently the Librarian at the En'owkin Centre and taking Linguistic courses at the En'owkin Centre.

Don L. Birchfield is Chickasaw/Choctaw; a member of the Choctaw Nation of Oklahoma, a 1975 graduate of the University of Oklahoma College of Law, and a former editor of CAMP CRIER, published by the Oklahoma City Native American Centre. He is presently serving on the national advisory caucus for Wordcraft Circle of Native American Mentor & Apprentice Writers, and is a co-editor of the Winter, 1994 Native American special issue of CALLALOO. His work has appeared in Bischinik, Gatherings III, Wicazo Sa Review and the Native Press Research Journal.

Peter Blue Cloud/Aroniawenrate is a member of the Mohawk Nation at Kahnawake, Mohawk Territory. He has seven books published including Elderberry Flute Song (White Pine Press, 1989) and The Other Side of Nowhere (White Pine Press, 1991).

Sally-Jo Bowman graduated from Kamehemaha Schools for Hawaiian children, a private school perilously close in mission to the U.S. Indian schools of the period. Her recent articles and essays about Hawaiian issues have appeared in National Wildlife, Sierra, American Forests and Aloha magazines and in the Christian Science Monitor and Seattle Times.

Molly Chisaakay is from the Dene Tha' tribe. She speaks fluently in both Dene Tha' dialects, and spent the first eight years of her school years in the Assumption Indian Residential School. Her first poem about sexual abuse and wife abuse was published in Writing the Circle.

Frank Conibear is from the Lyackson Band (Coast Salish) on Valdez Island. He lives and grew up in Victoria, B.C. He is married with one young son. He is a teacher/counsellor at Esquimalt Secondary, working with the First Nation students primarily, and teaching native studies (a grade 10 Social Studies Course).

Dorothy Christian is an indigenous woman of the Okanagan-Shuswap Nations of British Columbia. Born and raised on the Spallumcheen reservation in the interior of British Columbia, she is the eldest of ten children. She has been involved in various organizations in various capacities including the Ontario Film Review Board (O.F.R.B.), "Beyond Survival: The Waking Dreamer Ends the Silence", The En'owkin Centre, Canadian Native Arts Foundation and the Canadian Museum of Civilization, Nishnawbe-Aski Nation. Dorothy is working on completing a double major in Political Science and Religious Studies in the Honours Program at the University of Toronto.

Pamela Dudoward is a T'simshian poet who lives in Vancouver. She has an educational background in psychology, and has extensive work experience in employment counselling. Ms. Dudoward has developed and delivered workshops in job search and career planning. She is currently employed by the Ministry of Social Services.

Valerie Dudoward is a writer from the Tsimshian Nation who makes her home in Vancouver. Her plays have been staged by Spirit Song Theatre of Vancouver and Potlatch Theatre in Victoria. Ms. Dudoward's three-act play, Teach Me The Ways of the Sacred Circle, has been published in school textbooks by Gage Publishers and McGraw-Hill Ryerson Ltd. Her poetry has appeared in various anthologies, including Women and Words: The Anthology. She is currently employed by Native Courtworker & Counselling Association of B.C. as program co-ordinator of First Nations Focus, a career-planning 8 week learning experience.

Jim Dumont has pursued the cultural and spiritual roots of the traditional Indigenous North American Ways since 1970. From 1974, this pursuit has involved him thoroughly in the exploration, participation and learning of the Ojibway-Anishinabe Midewiwin Tradition, which has resulted in the achievement of 2nd Degree Midewiwin, sweatlodge rites, ceremonial leadership, and traditional-teacher responsibility. Since 1975, Mr. Dumont has been a professor of Native Studies at the University of Sudbury of Laurentian University in Ontario, Canada. He is one of the founders of the Department and has served four years as its Chair from 1984 to 1988.

Marilyn Dumont is Métis who writes from the experience of being native, woman and lower class. Dislocated from the Alberta Métis Settlements and her ancestors, she grew up first, in logging camps where her parents worked and second, in a small southern Alberta farming community. She is committed to working in the native community, where she has worked for 10 years in the areas of education and employment. She is presently working as a freelance writer and film maker.

Jack Forbes, Director of Native American Studies at the University of California, his tribal affiliations are Delaware-Lenpa and Powhantan-Renape. His latest book is entitled Columbus and Cannibals.

Forrest A. Funmaker is a Wisconsin Winnebago/Saulteaux now residing in Penticton. He is currently working on a project called *Tales from the Trail: Inside the World of Pow-Wows,* and is also working on a book of poetry and essays.

William George is Salish from the Burrard Reserve near Vancouver, and is nephew of the late Chief Dan George. He is currently a student at the En'owkin International School of Writing.

Monica Goulet is a Métis Woman of Cree, French and Saulteaux ancestry who is originally from the community of Cumberland House, Saskatchewan. She wrote a story called "KIAM" (Cree for "let it be") which is a tribute to her mother. It is being published in an anthology entitled Sharing Our Experience by the Canadian Advisory Council on the Status of Women. Monica's writing has also been featured in Briarpatch , New Breed and the SICC (Saskatchewan Indian Cultural Centre) - Profiles of Professional Aboriginal People in Saskatchewan.

Pamela Green LaBarge is currently pursuing an M.A. in Creative Writing at the University of WI-Milwaukee. She is on leave of absence from the Oneida Tribal School where she was employed as a Library Media Specialist. She is an enrolled member of the Wisconsin Oneida Tribe.

Leona Hammerton is a member of the Shuswap Nation, she is a graduate of the En'owkin International School of Writing.

Arthur John Harvey is a Oglala Lakota (Sioux) and a Creative Writing Major at the Institute for American Indian Arts. He will be attending the University of Montana in fall '93. He is also published in *Talking to the Sun and It's Not Quiet Anymore*.

A.A. Hedge Coke is (mixed) Huron/Tsa la gi/French Canadian and Portuguese. He is a graduate of the Institute of American Indian Arts. He is also published in *Voices of Thunder*, *It's Not Quiet Anymore*, *Caliban*, *Bombay Gin*, *Exit Zero*, *Naropa Summer Magazine*, *Talking to the Sun*, *Poetic Voices*, *Sparrowgrass*, *Anthology O* and *The Little Magazine*.

Peter Wayne Hill was born into the Wolf Clan of the Upper Mohawks, at the Oshweken Reserve near Brantford, Ontario. Wayne was raised on the reservation in the traditional Iroquois way, and exhibits a kindness and gentleness toward people known to Mohawk Peacekeepers. He has currently held his position as the Executive Director of the Fort Erie Native Friendship Centre for the past 12 years.

Trina Horne was born in Seattle, Washington. She is a Coast Salish native from the Tsawout Reserve of the Saanich Nation. She is employed as a Native Alcohol and Drug Counsellor for the Tseycum Reserve.

Blair Horsefall is a full blood Anishinabe. He has a Bachelor of Arts degree in Psychology and Indian Studies from the University of Regina, Saskatchewan.

LeAnne Howe is a Choctaw author, playwright and poet. Her work has been published in several American Indian anthologies including: Spider Woman's Granddaughters, Beacon Press (1989); American Indian Literature, The University of Oklahoma Press, Revised Edition (1991); Fiction International #20 (1991); Looking Glass, Publications in American Indian Studies (1991); Reinventing the Enemies Language, The University of Arizona Press (expected Fall, 1993); Earth Song, Sky Spirit: An Anthology of Native American Writers, Doubleday and Co. (expected Fall, 1993); and Studies in American Indian Literature, The University of Arizona Press, (expected Fall, 1993), as well as various poetry journals.

Jane Inyallie is of Carrier heritage. She is attending En'owkin for the second year in Creative Writing. Her occupation before going to school was Drug and Alcohol Counsellor.

Carrie Jack is Okanagan from Penticton, B.C., and has completed her first year of school at the En'owkin Centre.

Roger Jack is a member of the Confederated Tribes of the Colville Reservation. He was born and raised in Nespelem, Washington. His educational degrees include an Associate of Fine Arts degree in Creative Writing from the Institute of American Indian Arts in Santa Fe, New Mexico. He now works at Paschal Sherman Indian School in Omak, Washington, teaching Creative Writing and Indian Literature to young Indian students.

Wayne Keon, a member of the Ojibway Nation, he is a well-known author of Native literature and poetry. A business administration graduate, he is also a painter and financial analyst.

Sandra Laronde is an Anishnawbe kwe Temagami, Ontario. She graduated from the University of Toronto with an Honours B.A. in 1988 and studied at the University of Granada in Spain in 1989. She was one of the 1991 recipients of "CIDA" Professional Award which is funded by the Canadian International Development Agency for international education.

Mary Lawrence is an Okanagan from the Westbank Indian Band in BC, and is a graduate of the En'owkin International School of Writing. She recently published her first book of poetry entitled In Spirit and Song.

Duncan McCue is Anishinabe from Georgia Island, Ontario. He is currently working for the T.V. Program "YTV News" as a reporter.

Victoria Lena Manyarrows is Eastern Cherokee. She was raised alongside reservations and within mixed communities in North Dakota and Nebraska. Currently an arts administrator, since 1981 she has worked extensively with community arts and alcohol/substance abuse programs in the San Francisco Bay Area, and has a Master's degree in Social Work (MSW). Her essays and poetry have been published in various Native and multicultural publications in the United States and Canada, including the anthologies Without Discovery: A Native Response to Columbus, Piece of My Heart, Gatherings III: The En'owkin Journal of North American First Peoples and Voices of Identity, Rage and Deliverance.

Teresa Marshall is an urban Mi'kmaq living in Nova Scotia. Born between two worlds, she has necessitated an intense and critical exploration of her identity which she explores through writing, artmaking, theatre and research. She has exhibited her artworks throughout Canada, participates as a cultural researcher and educator in her community and will publish her first written works in Kelusultiek, an anthology of east coast Native women writers.

Patricia A. Monture-Okanee (Trisha) is a citizen of the Mohawk Nation, Grand River Territory. She is the mother to Justin, Blake and Kate and has married into the Thunderchild First Nation (Cree) in Saskatchewan. She currently resides in Ottawa with her family. Although a law professor by profession, Patricia considers herself to be a storyteller and has had the opportunity to speak in a variety of forums. She is a committed activist and author in matters of criminal justice, social justice, children's rights, and Aboriginal women's issues. All her work emphasizes the reality that her heart rests with her people, the First Nations.

Daniel David Moses, is a Delaware poet and Playwright from the Six Nations lands on the Grand River in Southern Ontario. His publications include the play Coyote City (Williams and Wallace 1990), and the book of poems The White Line (Fifth House 1990) and was the co-editor of An Anthology of Canadian Native Literature in English (Oxford 1992).

James A. Nicholas is from the Cree Nation. He is presently studying and working as an actor in Vancouver.

Michael J. Paul-Martin, a Cree from James Bay in Northern Quebec, is a former Trent University Native Studies student and a graduate of the En'owkin International School of Writing.

Sandra Power is a Siouxteaux native from the Musquepetung reserve, which is located near the Qu'appelle Valley in Saskatchewan. She recently graduated from the U.C.E.P. course at Concordia College in Edmonton, Alberta.

Louise Profeit-LeBlanc is northern Tutchone from the Yukon. She is a mother, grandmother, storyteller, poet and writer. Her main interest is working with Elders and grandchildren.

Odilia Galvan Rodriguez is Lipan Apache/Chicana originally from the south side of Chicago; Odilia has been a political activist and writer since age 15. She is co-founder and facilitator of Indigenous Women's Writing workshop, and a member of Centro Chicano/ Latino de Escritoires and Turtle Island Ensemble. She currently lives with her seven year old son Hawk, in Berkley, California. Her writings have appeared in several magazines and literary journals. Odilia is currently editing a poetry anthology of Chicano/Latino writers, completing work on a book of short stories and giving poetry readings nationally.

Armand Garnet Ruffo is a member of the Ojibway Nation. An alumus of the Writing Program at Banff Centre School of Fine Arts, he holds an Honours Degree in English Literature at University of Ottawa, and an M.A. from the University of Windsor.

J.C. Starr is half Gitksan on her father's side and half Sekani from her mother's side. She was born in Hazelton, B.C. She is presently enrolled at the Gitksan-Wet'suwet'en School of Journalism in Hazelton, B.C.

April Stonechild is Plains Cree from Saskatchewan. She is fifteen years old and considers writing her favourite pastime.

Doug S. Thomas is Saulteaux (Ojibway). He is a former journalist now working in the Public Relations field.

Jennifer Tsun is a mixed blood Algonquin living in rural eastern Ontario. She has been writing poetry and short stories for many years and has had numerous articles published in the alternative and local media. Jennifer is also a traditional wild rice gatherer at Ardoch, Ontario.

Carlson Vicenti is a member of the Jicarilla Apache tribe from Dulce, New Mexico. His works have been published by the Institute of American Indian Arts in Santa Fe, New Mexico, and Navajo Community College. He is currently a student at the En'owkin International School of Writing.

Gerry William is a member of the Spallumcheen Indian Band. He currently teaches English and Creative Writing classes at the En'owkin Centre in Penticton, B.C. He is also working on the second book of a trilogy entitled "Enid Blue Starbreaks", a space fiction set in the far future.

Spencer Touchie is from the Nuu-chah-nulth Tribal Area, and is a member of the Ucluelet Band, which is situated on the West Coast of Vancouver Island. He is eleven years old, born January 28, 1982. He will be starting the 6th grade this September, in Ucluelet Elementary School.

Richard Van Camp is from the Dene Nation in the North West Territories. He is a graduate of the En'owkin International School of Writing, and is currently involved in script writing for the CBC production North of 6O.